"I like my privacy," Desmond said, his words clipped.

"I bet you like being not dead better," she retorted. "Deal with it."

He said something that she pretended not to hear, then slid the tracking bracelet onto his wrist. A ping sounded from Remi's phone as it connected. "It's waterproof. If you take it off, I'll get an immediate alert to my phone, and I'll be at your last location in minutes, guns blazing. I've been known to ruin birthdays and romantic evenings, so don't take it off."

He didn't respond, but he wasn't stupid enough to test her. At least she didn't think he was.

Remi reached into the glove box and handed him a slip of paper. "My number. If I call, you answer. Otherwise, I assume the worst and—"

"Guns blazing," he interrupted, eyes on his phone. "So you said."

Prosecution's Protection

by

Michele Leech

Prosecution's Protection

Cover Art by *Kim Mendoza*

The Wild Rose Press, Inc.
PO Box 708
Adams Basin, NY 14410-0708
Visit us at www.thewildrosepress.com

Publishing History
First Edition, 2022
Trade Paperback ISBN 978-1-5092-4251-1
Digital ISBN 978-1-5092-4252-8

Published in the United States of America

Dedication

To my husband, who encouraged me to keep writing.
To Kaycee, who took a chance.
To CC, who inspired.

Chapter One

Desmond Graves long ago learned that gunshots didn't sound like they did in the movies. They weren't this loud, percussive explosion. More of an irritating popping sound, and despite knowing that, when he heard it walking to the door of his building, he still thought it was just some shit kids with fireworks.

Of course, the pain that exploded in his left arm and chest made him rethink that.

He remembered hitting the asphalt outside his apartment, blood filling his mouth as his teeth nearly went through his lip. He cursed himself for forgetting, even for a second, what his life was like.

The next thing he knew, he was waking up in a hospital room.

Rick O'Brien, an immovable force of spite and liquor, was sprawled over the single chair, making it look tiny under his massive form. His head was shaved, making the scars that lined his neck all the more obvious. With his pale gray eyes, scarred knuckles, and serious demeanor, very few could look at Rick and not tell him everything he wanted to know. Which worked well for Desmond.

The lack of light from the window made it clear it was either very late the same evening, or an entire twelve hours later. Neither of those was a preferable option. "What happened?" he asked as he tried to sit up.

"You got shot," Rick rumbled. His wide shoulders strained the fabric of his jacket. His gruff voice added to his intimidation. "Like I said you would."

Desmond tried and failed to take in an entire breath. "How bad is it?"

"Missed your lung. By that much." Rick held his thick fingers barely apart. "You got lucky."

Pressing his hand against his chest, Desmond tried to swing his legs to the side of the bed. Before he moved more than an inch, pain lanced through him and forced him back against the pillow.

His friend stared at him for a long, long moment. "You gonna give this shit up?"

"I'm not giving up anything." Desmond's weak voice irritated him. "They'd only try this if I'm getting close to something—"

"Well, *they* just got close, Graves! What about that police protection you were supposed to have?"

Desmond rolled his eyes and Rick sighed. "Figures."

They both knew that Corner City Police Department was too underfunded to maintain decent protection on him 24/7. And with the number of death threats he'd gotten, it made sense that they couldn't keep up on them all.

Adding to it that little incident where Desmond prosecuted one of the boys in blue, certain shifts on the force didn't care to keep up with the protection. Such was the life of Corner City's most infamous prosecutor.

"I need to make some phone calls," Rick said, getting to his feet. "Rest up. I'll be outside, so no one should try to kill you in the next fifteen minutes."

"Comforting," Des muttered, trying not to show

how exhausted he was as he leaned back.

"Go to sleep, boss," Rick repeated. "I'll take care of this." He shut the door, and Desmond could hear him talking into his phone quietly.

Despite the differences in their sizes, backgrounds, careers, and tax brackets, Rick O'Brien had been Desmond's closest friend his entire life. Rick had bounced around from job to job for quite some time, some more legal than others, before Desmond had gotten him a position as an investigator at the office. Rick enjoyed the hands-on work, and the opportunity for a little feather-ruffling was always available.

A buzz coming from his left had Desmond reaching for his phone—gunshot or not, work was work. Before he could touch it, Rick opened the door. "You touch that phone, and I'll throw it through the wall."

Desmond stopped. Not because he feared the threat, but because the last three times Rick had followed through with it. He didn't have time to transfer all of his data over yet again. "Fine."

He reclined back on the pillows and closed his eyes, fully intending to fake it until Rick was gone. The joke was on him, however, because soon Rick was slamming open the door and the room was much brighter. Blinking at the light, he sat up. "What time is it?"

"Just past nine. The doc says you can get sprung after eleven."

He looked at the large coffee cup Rick had passed him and was bitterly disappointed to find only water. As the muzziness cleared from the pills the nurses pushed on him last night, Des recalled the doctor coming in at some point. They'd reviewed his discharge instructions, and given him a printed copy, along with a business card. They included numbers for a psychiatrist for the possible long-term effects from the trauma and instructions for his follow-up.

"Thanks." He took a sip of tepid water, hoping it might ease the dryness in his throat. "Did you grab—"

The rest of the question stopped cold when without warning a woman appeared in the doorway. Leaning on the jamb, she obviously listened to their conversation. Long blonde hair hung past her shoulders, the dark gray cargo pants tucked into scuffed boots. A white tank top, covered with a black leather jacket opened just enough for Desmond to see the holster at her hip. Bright blue eyes stared openly at him, no shame in being caught, and the smirk on her face was clearly at his expense.

"Can I help you?" he asked, his voice dropping in temperature.

The grin widened. "You've got it backward."

"Come again?"

"I'm here to help you," she clarified, stepping into the room and closing the door. "Thought you were some brilliant lawyer—or something."

Doing his best to control his temper, Desmond turned to Rick. "Care to explain?"

Rick crossed his arms, already on the defensive, which wasn't a great sign. "You continuously choose the jobs with the biggest threats. You aren't gonna stop. Cops aren't gonna do shit."

"I've been getting threats for years."

"Yeah, but this time, someone's following through with it!" Rick shouted. "I can't be there all the time, and even if I could, I don't know what the hell to watch out for. You need protection."

Desmond waved one arm at the girl—woman—who couldn't be more than twenty-two. He felt ancient just looking at her. "You're joking."

Rick's brow arched while the girl smiled coldly. "See how much I'm not laughing," she said, gesturing at her face.

"How the hell are you supposed to do anything about this?" Desmond asked. "You're a little girl."

"First of all, you prick," she said, stepping forward and raising one finger, "your man hired me, so I shouldn't have to defend myself to you. Second," another finger went up, "sexism is out. Being a woman doesn't mean I can't kick your ass. Third, I'd do something about this by making sure your arrogant ass isn't left without protection from whoever you're pissing off and keeping you from doing something completely asinine, like getting shot. Oh." She put her hand down. "You already did that."

Desmond's smile was tight and without humor as he turned to Rick. "You don't see a problem with this?"

Rick shrugged, half-heartedly. "You can't get police protection, not enough of it, not after Everett."

Desmond's smile vanished at the mention of his father, but Rick continued, "You need someone to watch your back. She works with Cam at Exceptional Security, and this is what they do."

"She's a child," Desmond argued.

"Standing right here," she reminded him.

"I don't have time to watch out for her, too," Desmond continued, ignoring her.

"If this is you watching out for yourself, do I have my work cut out for me," she retorted.

"You know what," Desmond said, his temper snapping, "no one asked for you to be here—"

"He did," she retorted sharply, pointing at Rick. "And if you get your head out of your ass, you crooked spoon, you'd see he's got a point! You're in the goddamn hospital with a goddamn gunshot wound. Not a great sign that you can handle this."

Desmond stared at her, mouth agape in amazement at the insults, the attitude, and the actual valid points she presented. None of that made his temper ebb.

She took a step toward him. "You don't have to like it, but you'll pay me a ton of money and I'll keep you out of an early grave. Not only will I watch your arrogant ass, but I'll make it my mission to figure out who is doing this as quickly as possible, so we can both get back to our regularly scheduled lives. You survive; I get paid; everybody's happy."

He closed his mouth but couldn't come up with anything to say. She was right, and he hated it, but he didn't want to get shot again.

"All of this is moot anyway. I've already cashed your man's check, so you've got me through Friday as it is. You've got questions?" She pulled out a business card and threw it on his bed. "Call the number and they'll fill you in. I've got some shit to pick up, and I'll see you back here at eleven when you get sprung. We'll talk about the details then."

She turned on her heel and headed toward the door, and Desmond found his voice. "Who do you think you are?"

Facing him with a sarcastic grin, she said, "I'm Remi Archer, your personal protection service. Can't wait to work with you, Graves."

With a middle finger salute, she left the room, slamming the door behind her.

****

Remi waited outside the hospital, flipping her keys over her fingers. She never chose to drive the company car, but it only made sense this time. She couldn't transport the lawyer on her bike, her usual mode of transportation. Though, the idea of putting the puffed-up pompous ass on the back of her bike made her grin in wicked anticipation. She shelved that thought for another day.

Thomas Jones, her boss, had explained this assignment, adding with a dark look, "You are back on the roster, Archer."

She couldn't argue. Exceptional Security needed the money. And with Camille tied up with a client they called the 'historian,' and Samara dealing with the one known as the 'engineer,' it left Remi to bring in some bucks by protecting the lawyer.

She had yet to read the full file on him, but she'd heard of him before today. Mr. Desmond Graves was famous among the darker circles for taking down some of Corner City's biggest and nastiest bad asses. He'd actually convicted a few of the ones Remi had previous interactions with, including kingpin Arthur Small. Everyone had heard of him.

Though Graves had quite the fan club, the three death threats he'd received in the past week were all startlingly similar. Thomas had shown her them at the same time he handed over the file. Each contained a scarily close-up photo of Graves and various scribblings over the top in metallic ink.

Stop or you'll be sorry.

Drop the case or lose everything.

Do you care about your career more than your life?

Remi frowned. The words were so calm. Factual. The punctuation was perfect. These weren't the words of an unhinged individual, but a methodical and analytical mind. These weren't the usual, half-assed threats. These were promises.

The job itself was interesting, even if she'd hated the client on sight. He seemed like everything prosecuting attorneys were known to be: ruthless, soulless, heartless machines driven by money or glory. Desmond Graves seemed to fall in the latter category, his successes displayed on every paper in Corner City, criminal after untouchable criminal brought down in his courtroom. He played the jury like a fiddle and the criminals for fools and had the arrogance to go with it.

Remi looked up to see the hospital doors open. Rick O'Brien was carrying a bag, following an orderly who pushed the wheelchair holding an irritated looking Desmond Graves. She whistled to them, ignoring the glare Desmond cast in her direction.

She had to admit, for a jackass, he was handsome. Though he was dwarfed by Rick, he was still significantly taller than her, the close-cut hair not quite hiding the gray that was beginning to show. His eyes were striking, though his sullen glares were wasted on her. She also caught the shadows under his eyes that seemed to have been there long before this incident. He was dressed in dark slacks and a rumpled white shirt, left unbuttoned enough to expose the line of his throat. She wasn't one for expensive clothes, but she could admit he wore everything like it was made for him.

Which, considering his paycheck, it probably was.

She jerked her chin at the black car idling on the sidewalk. Rick followed her silent instructions, heading to the car to put Desmond's things inside. The orderly stopped the wheelchair by the door. Desmond stared up at her, the pallor on his face not diminished by the scowl. "I have a car."

"Wonderful," she said, ignoring him. "Here's your new bling." She handed him a silver bracelet.

"You're joking."

"I never joke about work." She glared at him. "That'll let me know where you are at all times."

When he simply put it in his pocket, Remi cocked a brow, intent on finishing that conversation soon. "We'll take my car and talk about the other rules. So get in."

"I'm not going anywhere until—"

Footsteps pounded the pavement rapidly behind her. Remi turned, her hand reaching toward her hip. An overly made-up brunette with eyes a little too hard charged at them. "Desi!" she shouted.

The tone made Remi believe she wasn't a threat. The tight top and jeans made it clear the woman wasn't carrying a weapon. And unless she was versed in six forms of unarmed combat, wasn't a danger to Remi. Which meant she wasn't a danger to her client.

The same client, who, in the time it had taken her to make these observations, managed to stand and take one step out from behind her.

Remi stepped to the side as the girl ran up to stop in front of them. "What happened?" Her hands hovered over his arms, like she was unsure of where to touch him without causing him harm.

"I'm fine. Just a little accident," he said, his tone

far nicer than the one he used when he addressed Remi. His face softened, and he automatically leaned over her in a protective stance, even though he was the one with a gunshot. Something in Remi relented.

The girl frowned. "*Little accident*?" she echoed, looking behind him to Rick. The big guy shrugged, keeping his mouth closed.

"It's nothing, Ash." Desmond squeezed one of her hands. "I'm fine."

As the young woman caught Remi's eyes, she cleared her throat. "Sorry. I'm Ashley Graves, Desi's sister."

"Nice to meet you," Remi said, nodding politely.

Desmond glared at her. "This is my new protection, thanks to Rick."

"Protection?" Ashley said, stifling a laugh.

Remi's smile was sharp, but she'd heard it all before. "Yup."

"Well," she said, looking Remi up and down. "Hopefully you know what you're doing."

"I do. Speaking of which, we need to go." She gestured to the car.

Desmond sighed, then turned back to his sister. "You take the bus here?"

"No, a friend dropped me off on his way to work."

Taking his keys out of his pocket, he held them in front of her, but didn't drop them into her palm. "You're going to drive Rick home. You get one scratch on it, and I'll never let you look at it, let alone drive it, again. Clear?"

Ashley nodded eagerly, reaching for the keys. Desmond pulled them away, and Remi saw how that motion made his eyes tighten in pain. "It better be parked in my spot before eight tomorrow morning."

"It will be," Ashley promised.

Desmond dropped the keys, then got into the agency car. Remi nodded once at Ashley and Rick, then got into the driver's side and started it up.

Though it wasn't her bike, Remi did love this car. Bulletproof glass, reinforced chassis, a veritable armory in the trunk, and it drove like a dream. She pulled out of the hospital parking lot, the quiet hum of the tires against pavement the only sound in the car for a couple of minutes.

"I don't need a tracker," Desmond said suddenly.

Remi didn't blink. "Fine. Then I'll stick by your side every moment of the day and night, until your stalker is caught. Your choice."

He muttered something, no doubt pithy, under his breath. "If I wear it?"

"I'll be at your side when you leave your apartment in the morning. I'll return you there at night. Any lunch meetings that are conducted outside of your place of business, I'm there. If you remain at work after the regular security goes home, I'll be joining you in your office until you decide to leave. Any place you go other than your place of residence or business, I'll be there."

These were standard rules for any security job. She'd already had Alec Singh, former client and now their technical services expert, pull the records of every coworker and every neighbor in Graves's apartment building. They were all clean enough. The security at his job wasn't fantastic, but it merely meant she'd be spending her days outside the Criminal Courts Building. At least it was better than other places she'd been paid to loiter outside.

"I like my privacy," Desmond said, his words clipped.

"I bet you like being not dead better," she retorted. "Deal with it."

He said something that she pretended not to hear, then slid the tracking bracelet onto his wrist. A ping sounded from Remi's phone as it connected. "It's waterproof. If you take it off, I'll get an immediate alert to my phone, and I'll be at your last location in minutes, guns blazing. I've been known to ruin birthdays and romantic evenings, so don't take it off."

He didn't respond, but he wasn't stupid enough to test her. At least she didn't think he was.

Remi reached into the glove box and handed him a slip of paper. "My number. If I call, you answer. Otherwise, I assume the worst and—"

"Guns blazing," he interrupted, eyes on his phone. "So you said."

"I'll check in with you periodically throughout the day. A quick text is all I need."

"I don't text."

She bit her lip and ignored that, getting off the highway and slowing down. "You'll need to get me a copy of all of your most recent case files. We'll look through them to figure out who is targeting you."

"I don't have any current cases," he said, in a tone that meant he wouldn't be doing any of what she asked.

"Look, Graves," she started.

"No, you look," he interrupted, his voice tight. "I don't care what Rick says. I don't need protection. Return whatever he paid you and—"

"Nonrefundable. And I'm not reneging on a contract." Although right now, she'd love to walk away and let whatever was going to happen, happen.

"I don't know who you usually work for but—"

"I work for people who are interested in staying alive, Graves!"

"I'm not upending my life because Rick is overprotective."

"Well, he paid me, so I'll ask again if you fucking understand—"

He looked at her, those unnervingly calm eyes stared at her through the dim light of the cloudy sky. "I understand this is a contract. When the money is up, your time is done. When are you paid through?"

"Through Friday," Remi bit out.

"Fine. Then on Friday, we'll be saying goodbye."

"Fine by me, you walnut."

The rest of the drive went in complete silence. She parked outside of his building, then walked him up to, of course, his penthouse suite. He fumbled for the keys, and if he hadn't been such a prick, maybe she would have helped him. As it was, he got in, then shut the door in her face without another word.

Remi flipped off the door as she heard the deadbolt slid into place, then returned to the car. A different sound than the ping from the tracker echoed from her phone. She opened the email from Thomas to find Desmond's file.

Turning the radio up, she started skimming through it, wishing it was Friday so she didn't have to learn anything more about this pretentious, arrogant, pain in the ass...

An hour later, she dropped the phone onto the passenger's seat with a sigh and rubbed her eyes. She'd learned quite a bit from the file on Desmond Graves.

More than she'd wanted to. After giving the charges brought against his father one last thought, she pulled out into the street.

If they kept going the way they were, Desmond Graves wasn't going to want her help by the end of the week, and he needed it.

Worse, he deserved it.

Despite his knee-jerk reaction to her, she didn't think it was her gender that he had a problem with. Perhaps her age. Maybe her perceived lack of experience. Maybe he was just so used to doing everything alone.

She had a bad attitude, she knew. Her coworkers had learned how to deal with her, but it took time. He clearly had a temper, too. But she recalled the list of people he'd put away, and the obvious lengths he would go through to get a rightful conviction, the way he looked at his little sister...

Maybe...just maybe, they'd gotten off on the wrong foot.

Remi Archer had never lost a client. She wasn't about to start now. If her usual methods didn't work, she'd have to adjust. Gripping the steering wheel tighter, she made a silent promise to try a different tactic tomorrow.

Chapter Two

Desmond cursed through his teeth as his wound pulled for the third time that morning. Dropping his hand, he gave up on the idea to grab for the travel mug from the top shelf, deciding to stop for his morning coffee on the way to the office instead. He usually bought coffee only on Fridays, but today, he'd make an exception. He checked his shirt, relieved that he hadn't bled through again. Grabbing his coat in one hand and his briefcase in the other, he glared at the flash of silver at his wrist.

Remi Archer had dropped him off last night like a toddler for a playdate. She walked him to his door as if he were completely incapable of caring for himself. Granted, his current situation tended to suggest that, but it was one incident in a ten-year career. He hated being seen as weak, and to have someone like her assigned to protect him.

As he shook his head and headed out, the door locked automatically and the deadbolt slid into place with a metallic whirr. Just because this was the first time he'd been injured didn't mean it was the first time he'd thought of taking precautions.

After his mother passed, his portion of the trust she'd left him had been invested. He'd withdrawn enough to buy his penthouse and put in security systems, while still leaving enough to accrue while he continued to work. Between his salary, pension, and the rest of the trust, he wouldn't have to worry about what he'd do after retiring. If he made it that far.

Though he didn't usually take the elevator, he indulged himself for once. The floors ticked down from seven before opening on the lobby level. With a nod to his doorman, Peter, he stepped out the door and nearly walked right into a short blonde.

"Excuse me, I—" The automatic apology broke off when Remi grinned up at him. "Dammit, I thought—"

"That I'd forget?" She shrugged, clothed in much the same style as yesterday. "Sorry to disappoint. Coffee?" She held out a tall cup. Behind her shoulder, he saw an unfamiliar motorcycle parked at the curb. The leather jacket made more sense now.

He took the cup hesitantly, ignoring the fragrant aroma of freshly ground beans, his frown fixed in place. "What's this for?"

"I stopped to get my own. Guessed that you just like it black, 'cause you seem straight-laced like that." Her gaze was teasing, with none of the anger or judgment she'd had yesterday. When he just took a silent sip, she nodded. "Thought so. Don't get used to it. I was running late. From now on, you're getting your own damn coffee. You aren't paying me the big bucks to do your caffeine runs."

"I'm not paying you anything."

"You wouldn't want Rick's money to go to waste, would you?" she retorted rapid fire and jerked her chin at the street. "Let's go. Don't wanna be late."

Desmond fell into step beside her, heading toward the sidewalk. Remi didn't seem to be surprised that he walked to work, but he supposed it was all compiled into some sort of file on him.

"How'd you sleep?" she asked, sipping her drink.

He wasn't about to tell her he'd split open his wound three times during the night. Twice he thought he'd heard gunshots in his room, and once, the sound of someone coming in through his door. All of them had been nothing more than an overactive imagination, but as a result, he'd spent more time dressing his wound than sleeping.

"Fine," he lied, taking another sip of his coffee. "Were you waiting long?"

"Nope. Why? Planning on ducking out earlier tomorrow to avoid the inevitable?"

He'd considered it. "Not anymore."

She laughed, tipping her cup back and, in the process, taking a step nearer to him and forcing him to move closer to the buildings and away from the sidewalk. He was about to call her out on not being able to drink and walk at the same time when a man in the car on the edge of the sidewalk swung the passenger door open. It would have slammed right into Remi, and he would have been face-to-face with whoever was in there. This way, she stayed between them.

Desmond frowned, drinking his coffee and using it as an excuse to watch his...bodyguard a little closer. She'd taken the outside of the sidewalk, putting herself next to cars and the street. Though she disguised it by drinking her coffee and tossing her hair to the side, her eyes were constantly moving, checking those around, above, and behind them without being obvious. As people approached, he watched the way she scanned them each before moving on, categorizing them in some way only she understood.

He was suddenly curious as to how this short, bad-tempered blonde got into something like taking care of other people. Besides, if she could try to be civil, so could he. It would make the week go by faster. "How did you end up as a bodyguard?"

She didn't look up at him. "My dad was a cop. Then he got political, and we traveled around for a while. Lived on a bunch of different military bases. Always around guns, security, and piss poor excuses for soldiers. When I was old enough, I trained with the Israeli Defense Force. Did some border patrol in Jordan Valley with some badass women. After that, I joined a private company." Something about the way she said it made him think it wasn't quite above board, but he didn't comment. "When I quit, I came back here and fell into the security gig."

He thought he'd detected a hint of an accent. "And you've had experience in something like this before?"

"Stalkers?" She looked up at him. "Yeah. A couple of runs of that. Also, a little fieldwork tracking down people. I've served as personal protection. That's why my boss chose me for this job. Uniquely qualified."

"Stalkers aren't exactly anything new to you."

"Yours is."

He knew why he thought so, having seen several levels of scumbags before, but he wanted to gauge her response, her skills. "How?"

Remi took another long sip from her cup, eyeing a man over the rim until he crossed the street away from them. As they approached the Criminal Courts Building, Desmond slowed his steps slightly, waiting for her response.

"The ones I've met are messed up. Obsessive. Off-kilter. They end up getting caught because of that obsession." She stopped, looking up at his building. "Your guy doesn't seem the type to mess up. His letters are careful. The attack was planned. This isn't usual behavior, and usual methods won't work."

Desmond turned to face her, watching her expression as she eyed him, like she was searching for something. "How do you see this turning out?" he asked, finding himself, in an annoying way, in agreement with her.

She continued to stare, nodding a little before she answered. "I don't think we'll find him before he attacks again. He's out to get you, and even though he's made damn sure you know he's coming, we've got nothing on him. He's good." She looked past him, then back to meet his eye. "It's gonna be you or him."

Desmond looked at her for a moment, then down at his watch. She hadn't lied to him. Nor had she tried to placate him with hollow words that he knew were wrong. He appreciated that. He still didn't want the protection, but he was beginning to understand why she'd been chosen.

Remi seemed to know the conversation was over. She nodded toward the entrance door of his office building. "See you later."

Desmond didn't bother to say goodbye, but turned and walked toward the practice, the reassuring weight of a blue gaze on his back the entire way.

****

Though he hadn't missed any working days due to his "incident," Desmond still felt like he'd fallen behind. He usually worked ten to twelve hours every day, regardless of if it was a weekend or not. So he worked straight through the morning and well into the afternoon before the caffeine headache set in. Needing an extra jolt other than what the ancient office coffee maker could provide and wanting to get out of the building for at least a few minutes, he grabbed his coat and wallet and headed to the elevators.

Despite being back on his feet, he wasn't nearly as observant as he should have been. Desmond had to stifle a sigh as a young brunette jumped up from her seat and joined him in the elevator.

Stacy Richards wasn't the first intern to develop a crush on him, but she was one of the more persistent ones. Always cautious never to put himself in a situation where someone could get leverage over him, he'd avoided being alone with the younger interns, just in case. He'd seen firsthand how bloodthirsty his coworkers could be and wouldn't put it past some of them to use it to their advantage.

However, Stacy dogged him like no one before. She always managed to walk past his office when he looked up, passed him on the way to the restroom, waltzed into work at the same time, and left at the same time. She'd even shown up at a few of his coffee haunts. She was cute enough, but it was becoming tiresome. He'd explained that he wasn't interested, trying to be polite, but that only seemed to drive her to try harder. Had it not been for her inane conversation and the inability to get through one court docket without a grammatical error, Desmond might have pegged her for his stalker.

"Coffee, Mr. Graves?" She didn't wait for his answer. "Me too. I've been working my way through some of your old cases." She stood close to him on the elevator, never minding that they were the only two in the large space. "They are just riveting."

He didn't respond, but took out his phone, scrolling through the new emails. Ignoring Stacy never made her leave, but at least he could get more work done.

"I heard you were in an accident over the weekend. If you need anything, I'm available any time, day or night. I can give you my number—"

The doors dinged open, and Desmond stepped through, Stacy hot on his heels. "You know, I don't live far from here. I can make you something nice and hot, and it'll all be on—"

"About time, thought you forgot."

Desmond looked up, finding Remi standing in their path. He was at a loss as to what she referred to. Hadn't he answered her texts every hour on the hour—especially after a second, more dangerously worded request came in via text?

Frowning slightly, he opened his mouth to respond, but Remi cut in. "I wasn't sure if we were meeting here or the coffee shop to go over the case." Her eyes never once wandered to Stacy.

He almost smiled at her cleverness but smothered it. Stacy, unsurprisingly, spoke up. "Who are you?"

Only now did Remi look at her, somehow looking down despite the fact they were the same height. "A client. Who the hell are you?"

Stacy bristled, her eyes shocked at Remi's language. "Excuse you, I'm Mr. Graves's—"

"She's an intern," Desmond cut in. "Who has work to do somewhere else."

"But, Mr. Graves, I thought we were going—"

"Nowhere," he finished firmly.

She gaped up at him, her eyes darting between him and Remi before she crossed her arms, the artfully unbuttoned blouse straining. When Remi winked at her, she flushed in anger but didn't try to speak again.

Desmond started walking, ignoring Stacy as Remi fell into place beside him. Once they were far enough away, he glanced back, relieved that Stacy had gone back toward the elevator.

"So," Remi offered, "she seems nice."

He couldn't help his scoff of laughter and shook his head. "I think this is the first time I've been able to go out alone for coffee in months. Well—" He waved his hand at Remi, acknowledging the falsity of that statement.

She just grinned at him. "I'm not hearing a thank you, Mr. Prosecutor."

"And you won't."

She held the door for him as he stepped out, blinking at the sunlight. Remi was right behind him. "Aw, what's the matter? Rough day at the office?" she said, grinning, her eyes darting around the sidewalk.

"Something like that," he agreed, glancing at her.

Remi nodded. "So is this coffee shop a place you go often?"

"No. Never on Mondays, and I usually go to the one up the street. Farther away, so Stacy usually had to leave before long."

"Clever," she said, still watching the crowd. "Your fan's pictures came from that one, so we'll avoid it until he's caught."

"He knows where I live," Desmond said. "You think avoiding coffee is going to stop him?"

She reached the door of the shop first and opened it

for him. "Nope. But let's not make it easy for him."

Desmond stepped in, getting in the short line. When they got up to the counter, he said, "Large black coffee and a shot of espresso. And"—he gestured to Remi—"whatever she's having." He refused to acknowledge her grin and merely said, "We're even."

She didn't stop grinning, and Desmond felt his mouth curl up in response.

****

It was well after the usual lunch hour before Desmond left the building again to grab something to eat. Usually, he worked through lunch and just had a snack, but the wound was starting to pull and itch, and the generalized body weakness—which the surgeon had warned him about, but he'd ignored—wasn't helping him concentrate.

He brought the file for his most irritating case with him, hoping food would help him crack this, and intended to go to the small Indian restaurant. Three steps out and his face buried in the files, he was barely paying attention.

"Buying me lunch, now?" a voice said in his ear.

"Jesus—!" Desmond hated to admit that he flinched, a few of the papers dropping out of the folder.

Remi snatched them before they hit the ground, grinning widely as he got his breath under control. "For someone who thinks they don't need my help, you're pretty oblivious," she observed, glancing over the papers she held.

Desmond grabbed them. "You realize I spend most of my time around people who kill and murder for a living. I know how to get rid of a body."

Her smile was even larger this time. "Me too. So

where are we going for lunch?"

"Indian. Is that all right with you?"

"I'm more of a Thai girl, myself."

He looked back at the file, something sparking in his mind. "I don't actually care."

Remi grabbed his wrist and tugged him out of the way of a pedestrian. Desmond resisted the urge to wrench his hand away, the callouses on her fingers brushed along the scars on his wrist, sending sparks up his arm. She dropped her hand and made no comment.

Tucking the file under his arm, he continued down the sidewalk, eyes up, unsurprised when Remi fell into step with him. "Indian it is, then," she said, her smile and tone completely agreeable.

"I hate you."

She laughed but made no move to touch him again.

****

Over Indian food, Desmond watched Remi scroll through her phone without ever actually looking at it while keeping her focus on the diminishing crowd. They'd arrived after the lunch rush, so the staff chatted among themselves and gave them some privacy. "What do you do all day?" he asked, curiosity getting the better of him.

"This and that. Consultation in my spare time. Precincts email me with some issues, and I advise them. Mostly diplomatic security stuff. Nothing too exciting." She put the phone down and leaned back, the corner table she'd requested offered a great view of the room.

Desmond cut off another piece of chicken and chewed slowly, watching Remi. Her eyes scanned the room again, despite the few patrons, and that grin remained on her face.

"Why do you do that?"

"Do what?"

"That constant watching over your shoulder."

It made him anxious. He kept looking back at whatever she was noticing. But the few times he did, all he'd seen were the worn booth seats and empty tables. It was a narrow restaurant, longer than it was wide, and many of his coworkers were unaware of it. He'd found it by accident, just trying to find something that could keep him going through the evening. The staff was always polite and helpful, and often had his usual order going before he even asked for it.

Her brow arched as she picked at her plate of tandoori chicken. "Kind of the job."

He didn't buy that and said so.

"How do you feel about all this?" she asked, tearing apart a piece of naan with her fingers.

She wasn't asking about lunch. "Archer—"

"Humor me, Mr. Prosecutor."

He set his knife and fork down, quiet as the waitress came and refilled their glasses. When she left, he met Remi's eyes. "I hate it," he said honestly. "I hate not having privacy. I hate being watched. I hate not knowing what's going to happen."

Remi nodded, looking unsurprised by his answer. "I spent a lot of time living like that. So I learned how to spot them first. The people who'd hurt me or take advantage of me. I learned how to be the one in command of every situation. Spotting the threats, the exits, potential dangers. I learned how to use anything as a weapon, how to read people. I keep control. Because the alternative isn't something I'm gonna allow again."

"If this is you in control, I'm not sure I can handle you out of it."

She winked at him. "Oh, you absolutely can't, Graves."

He almost smiled but settled for a nod instead. As the waitress came by, Remi grabbed the check and threw a credit card down. "I got this one."

Desmond drank his water and eyed her over the glass, recognizing the faint and all too inconvenient feelings of respect coming forward for Remi Archer.

Dammit.

****

Remi stood up from the bench right outside the entrance to the Criminal Courts Building. Several of them lined the sidewalk leading up to it, and the one she'd been stuck on all day had a small tree to give some shade. She twisted and stretched out limbs that ached from hours of inactivity. She'd known ADA Graves would be a pain in the ass; she hadn't anticipated it being literal.

The sun had set several hours ago. The last stragglers of the Criminal Courts Building had headed out some time ago, and still no sign of Graves. She'd checked the tracker, he was still inside and answering her hourly check-ins, so she had no excuse to go in other than boredom. And since she was trying to play nice…

She sighed, pacing around the front of the building. The nice thing about being in this district was the people-watching. Made her job more challenging, but at least it kept her busy. This late, though, most everyone was heading home and wrapping up. She forced herself to pay attention to the empty streets, watching the light at the corner flicker.

The door opened behind her, and Remi turned, finally seeing Desmond exit. He noticed her with sunken eyes. "You here to tell me that you've caught my fan, and you'll be on your way?"

"If only," she answered easily, getting into step with him. She appreciated that he walked to and from his home—it allowed her to get some exercise in.

He sighed. "Damn."

They maintained a comfortable silence on the way back to his place. They passed the parking garage again and headed up to his penthouse suite, the elevator ride completely silent.

"Well," Desmond said, stopping outside his door. Exhaustion laced his voice in a way that wasn't there a few hours ago. He'd moved slower than he had this morning. Asshole needed to get some rest. "This has been thrilling. Looking forward to tomorrow."

"Same," she said, knowing he wasn't going to like what was coming next. "But it isn't goodbye just yet. I have to check your place."

"No."

Remi merely smiled and waited. Just as she had been all day, tense and ready. "I should have done it last night, but you shut the door in my face. That was a mistake on my part—one that won't happen again."

Desmond stared at her for a long moment then, pinching his brow, exhaled slowly. She stepped aside as he unlocked the door, revealing a cardboard box just inside the door as it opened.

Remi grabbed the handle and slammed it shut.

"Archer, what the—"

"Was that there this morning?"

Desmond stared at her, the obvious exhaustion rolling across his face as he tried to think. "No, I don't think so."

She kept her left hand on the door and the right on her holster. "Who has a key to your place?"

"The doorman, Rick, Ashley—Archer, it's a delivery," he argued. "Enough. I'll make sure they leave them downstairs from now on."

"Graves—"

"No." He stepped in front of the door. "No. You've made your point. It's been a long couple of days. I just want to go to bed."

"Graves, dammit, I'm trying here, but my job is to keep you alive. Can you do me the favor of letting me try?" she said, trying to control her temper as best she could.

He cursed under his breath and stepped back, leaving the key in the door. "Five minutes."

Remi stepped in, eyes casting over every perfect, immaculate surface, the baby grand piano in the corner of the open living room, the full decanters of what looked like alcohol. She toured the hallway, passed the empty master bedroom and guest room, and balcony, devoid of everything but a small patio set.

With an irritated wave from Desmond, she checked the box for any signs of tampering, shaking it slightly. There were no distinctive smells or unusual powders and weight to it. She peeled away the tape, revealing nothing more than a piece for his piano. She finally returned to the living room, where Desmond was placing his briefcase on his desk.

"I know you're upset, but this is what we have to do." Her nerves had spiked at the sight of the box, and she could feel her accent getting worse with the adrenaline. "Job means—"

He slammed his hands down on the table. "Archer, this so-called *job* has been blown way out of proportion. I don't need protection. I don't need a babysitter. I don't need you."

"Will you stop being such a stubborn ass and look around? You got shot, this is—"

Desmond snapped. "I'm well aware of what happened. I don't need you to treat me like a child."

"Then stop acting like one and let me do my job."

"I don't need your help, sweetheart. I've been looking out for myself and Ashley since before you were born."

Remi inhaled sharply, then stepped away, dropping her arms to her sides and forcibly relaxing her shoulders. He was right. Shouting at him wasn't going to convince him. But he had to be convinced because as much as she hated him sometimes, she was starting to like this dry-humored, sarcastic workaholic. She was silent for a minute, staring out at the picturesque view before she turned around.

"Okay, look. If you ever call me sweetheart again, I will punch you so hard you'll throw up for three days. Not a joke."

He rolled his eyes, either in humor or exasperation, she couldn't tell, then he slumped on the white leather couch, rubbing his eyes.

Remi followed, sitting on the coffee table in front of him. "Second, I get it. I do. This whole thing sucks, and the last thing you want is me coming in here and messing with your shit. But I need you to see this from my perspective, okay?"

"Archer—"

"Just…let me try to explain. If you don't want my help afterward, fine. We'll do it your way. But if you do, we'll try to do this thing right, okay? I'll do my best to stay out of your life, and you meet me halfway."

It was clear he didn't think she could say anything that could convince him. "Fine."

"Okay." She dropped her eyes and took a deep breath, trying to organize her thoughts. The fake wood floor was smooth beneath her scuffed boots. "There was this barista, Anna. She was being stalked. A shady creep who'd tracked her across the country. She went through everything with the police, just like she should have. Everything by the book. She took precautions. She wasn't stupid. Didn't take risks. A few years went by, and she thought she'd gotten rid of him."

Remi looked down at her hands, knowing that they'd usually be shaking. She kept her focus on her hands, trying to keep her voice detached. "She met a guy. Tim. Nice enough. Kind of a moron, but he made her happy. They moved in together. They were happy," she repeated, as if that would change the way she knew it ended.

"Archer—" Desmond's voice was quiet as if he knew where this was going.

She ignored him. "Her stalker found them and followed Tim back to their place one night. When Anna got home, Tim was already dead, in their bedroom, in pieces. And above the bed, in Tim's blood, her stalker had written her a love letter. That they were soulmates. That he was doing this for her." Remi watched her hands clench. "My first job at Exceptional Security was taking care of Anna after that. I caught the guy and made sure he wouldn't hurt her again, but I couldn't fix what he'd already done to her. I couldn't change what happened."

She looked up at him, needing him to understand. "It's horrible, what he did. But the thing is, he didn't think so. There are bad people, and there are monsters. You handle bad people all day, eyes shut, and that's amazing, honestly. I know you're good at it. But the guy after you is a monster. He wrote those letters, he knows where you work and get your coffee, and he attacked you where you live. I need you to realize I'm not here because you're incapable or weak or whatever other nonsense you think. I'm here because he's a monster, capable of terrible things, and taking down monsters is what I do."

Desmond said nothing for a long moment, and she prayed she'd gotten through to him. Lawyers might deserve a lot of awful things, but no one deserved monsters.

He got up suddenly, startling Remi as he strode into the kitchen. He grabbed the dark counter, hunching over it. She saw his back shudder, and red started to seep through his shirt.

"Shit, Desmond—" Remi stood, walking toward him. She would've said more, but he was pale, his teeth clenched, and his breath coming too quickly. She recognized that. "First aid?"

He jerked his chin to the side, and she found a bag of stuff from the hospital, with gauze and tape. Grabbing it, she turned back to him. "Come on, old man," she said, grabbing his shoulder. "Turn around. Let me see."

He allowed her to push him until he faced her. His

fingers shook as he unbuttoned his shirt. Remi kept talking, narrating everything and keeping her voice calm. "You've bled through your shirt and the bandages, so I've gotta rewrap it. You're running low on gauze. I can bring some tomorrow. Wow, didn't expect a lawyer to have abs. When the hell do you find time to work out? Just breathe. It's gonna be fine. You've been such a prick, I wondered if you were human at all, and now's the time you decide to prove me wrong, huh? What a great first day."

His breath started to even out, calming as she finished taping up the bandage. She didn't speak again until he was cleaned up and she stepped away. "It's okay, Graves."

He leaned against the counter, bloodied bandages next to him, eyes sunken in as he stared at her, and Remi felt her heart go out to this arrogant, cold, fiercely independent man.

"It isn't okay," he said quietly, the first admission he'd ever given her. The first real moment of fear. It shook Remi to see him looking nearly broken, and she couldn't stop herself from doing what she did next.

She reached out and squeezed his hand, her thumb running over the white knuckles; he didn't pull away like he had earlier. "You're right," she said. "It's not. It's fucked up."

The sound that escaped him wasn't a laugh, but it was close. His fingers wrapped around hers.

She squeezed a little tighter and stepped in. "I'm here now, and they're not gonna touch you. If you need me, say the word and I'm there, guns blazing. Anytime. I'm gonna keep you safe. I promise."

Chapter Three

Over the next few days, Desmond discovered quite a bit about Remi Archer. Every little piece of information he got, he filed away in an increasingly complicated pocket of his mind. Some things were small notes—she hated having her hair pulled up, even when it was more convenient. She loved her leather jacket more than most people loved their children. Other things were funny inconsistencies with her rough and tumble attitude. She wore thick, colorful socks beneath her boots. She couldn't handle spicy foods. She loved saying things that shocked people, be it by her language or blunt statements. She preferred whiskey to every other type of liquor.

Then there were those other things he noticed. In the dive of a Greek restaurant where they went for lunch on Wednesday, she saw bruises on their waitress's arm and pulled her aside, speaking in a low tone for a few moments. She checked his mail with annoying attention to detail. He noticed how when she got tired, her voice became rougher, and started to show a bit of an accent, maybe Middle Eastern?

He noticed that she touched him a little more—a hand at his back or his shoulder, brushing his hand when she took his bag from him so he could unlock the door to his penthouse. It didn't bother him, not really, but he was so unused to it that it startled him every time. She commented, merely smiled and kept doing it. After the first few days, he started to expect it. He no longer flinched. She didn't stop, and he started to look forward to those small moments.

For a long time, he'd fought and strived to make a reputation as one of the most serious, untouchable lawyers in the city, and he'd succeeded. People feared him or admired him, but they didn't try to get close to him. He'd encouraged it. He liked his space. It hadn't been until years later that he realized Rick was his only friend. Remi was hired to be here, but…he was starting to like having her around.

He noticed that when Remi smiled, the lines at the corner of her eyes deepened, erasing some of the years that seemed so incongruent on her face.

He noticed more than he probably should.

****

It was Thursday afternoon, just after lunch, when they were walking back to the office. He'd spent the morning in court hearings and had a meeting with the DA later in the afternoon. Remi enjoyed the change of pace, happy to leave the uncomfortable cement bench behind her.

Her mouth was still on fire from the lunch meal. When she asked for mild, she'd meant not at all spicy. Desmond had laughed, ordering her something called a mango lassi to quell the flames, but the smile remained. She'd chugged it, and though it helped, the residual burn was still there; her cheeks still burned like fire.

"Brought down by lamb vindaloo," Desmond drawled, that same rare smile on his lips. "Who would've thought?"

"You can't stab spicy," Remi argued, unable to

help her laugh in response.

"If you want spice, tomorrow, we'll do southern Indian."

His phone rang, not for the first time this lunch hour, and he pulled it out to look at the screen. Most of the calls he'd let go to voicemail, but Remi caught Ashley's name as he accepted this one and raised it to his ear. "Hello?"

Remi tucked her hands into her pockets, the chill of the fall air beginning to settle in. They got to the crosswalk, but as the light changed to cross, Desmond stood still, a frown appearing between his eyes. She stopped as well, not wanting to intrude, but knowing she had no choice.

"When did it happen?" he asked, looking past her. "Right. No, I'll handle the arrangements. Yeah. I know. I'll call you tomorrow with the details. Bye."

He hung up, his phone sliding back into his pocket before he cleared his throat. The light changed again, and Desmond crossed, staring ahead. When they got to the Courts Building, she couldn't stop her question. "Everything okay?" she asked, already knowing it wasn't.

"My father died in prison this morning. Heart attack." His voice was detached. "I have to make the arrangements for the funeral."

Remi reached out to him. "Shit, Desmond, I—"

"It's fine." He stepped away. "It'll mean a late night here, though. I want it done as soon as possible." He looked around the relatively barren sidewalk. "I know this isn't exactly thrilling, so—"

"Don't worry about me. If you need anything..." She trailed off, unsure of what else she could say.

"Thanks." He headed into the building, his head bowed as he entered, completely ignoring the greetings of the security guard.

As soon as he was out of sight, Remi pulled out her phone and dialed a number she really should have in her speed-dial. A polite, charmingly accented voice answered. "Exceptional Security, this is Gemma, how may I direct—"

"It's me."

The polite tone dropped a notch. "Miss Archer, Thomas expected a report yesterday."

"Yeah, well, Thomas can get off his flat ass and—"

"Was there something you wanted?" Gemma interrupted.

"Yeah. My client's father just died. I wanna make sure it wasn't something more."

"This would be Desmond Graves?" Gemma asked, the clicks of her keyboard audible in the background.

"Yeah. The father's name is Everett Graves, incarcerated six years ago." Remi leaned against the bench, her eyes darting over the crowds. She saw a familiar face, one that she'd expected to see earlier, and started moving toward it. "Call me when you get something."

"Will do, and, as always, a pleasure to—"

Remi hung up, jogging to intercept the large man. "Rick."

He turned, looking down at her from his impressive height. "Blondie."

"Remi."

"Don't care." Despite that, he stopped. "How's it going with Graves?"

"He's a pain in the ass, and straightlaced to the

point of suffocation, but I've got his back."

Rick chuckled. "That first night, I think he called you a sarcastic midget of curses and poor life choices."

Remi laughed aloud at that. "He wasn't wrong."

"Any news on Graves's fan?" Rick asked.

"Not yet." She didn't mention anything about his father; that wasn't her news to tell.

"I know he's a shit, but he doesn't deserve all this," Rick said quietly.

"I'll keep him safe."

He huffed, losing the sincerity. "Don't tell me you like the asshole?"

"You know, I kind of do," Remi said, grinning. "How's Camille?"

"Busy. We're meeting for drinks next week." He stretched. "Anyway, gotta get back to work. Enjoy your loitering, or whatever."

Remi waved him off and returned to her bench. A message came in from Gemma a few moments later.

—Everett Graves's autopsy revealed nothing more than he was a heavy smoker with a poor diet. All natural causes of death. No red flags.—

She was almost disappointed, not that she'd ever say it aloud. Still, this was a different issue, and she wasn't sure Desmond would let her help. The idea made her stomach twist a little. Shaking her head free, she continued to scan faces, focusing on the job. Because this was all just a job.

Just a job.

****

Desmond hung up the phone, his eyes starting to swim from exhaustion. Though he hadn't opened up his wound again since Monday, it didn't mean he was healed, and everything else on top of it was just…overwhelming.

He rubbed his temples, everything ready for the funeral on Saturday. The call from Ashley hadn't exactly been a surprise, but he hadn't anticipated it this week. There was no lost love between him and his father, not since their last visit. But he owed it to Ashley to give him a proper funeral. If only for Ashley.

Looking at the clock, he cursed, it was well past nine. He bent down, grabbing his bag from beneath his desk so he could get back downstairs to Remi and at least let her get some sleep before their early morning. He'd treat her to lunch tomorrow, though it was her turn. He couldn't remember the last time he'd gone out for lunch every day in a week, but the chance to relax was something he didn't usually go for. The conversations with Remi were stimulating, and he almost forgot that she'd been hired to spend time with him.

No, to protect him.

A strange thought occurred to him, what would she be doing if she weren't working for him? Did she go out for drinks with friends? Dancing? Did she have a significant other? A sharp, strange sensation began in his ribs when he thought of the idea of Remi going home to someone, but he ignored it, straightening and heading to his door to lock it.

As he put the key in the lock, he heard a creak of the floor behind him.

Even with the exhaustion, his mind was sharp and jumped to the obvious thoughts. It was late. No one else should be here. No one.

Desmond twisted as a hand grazed his arm, his

right hand immediately going up defensively. Remi caught his arm easily, but her brows rose in surprise. "Not bad, old man. You got some moves." She smiled tentatively. "Didn't mean to scare you."

"You didn't," he said, picking up his bag.

She smirked. "Unh huh. You ready?"

They walked back to his place, both of them quiet and lost in their thoughts. Remi didn't speak until they reached the parking garage. "I know my being here might cramp your style and all, but if you need to go out and get drunk with your friends, I can make that happen. If that's what you need."

"I'm fine. Not exactly my kind of scene."

They reached the elevator bank, and Remi pressed the button without asking. They usually took the stairs, but he was too exhausted to even think about climbing all those flights.

"What is your kind of scene?" she asked. "Do you go out with Rick or anything?"

He shrugged as the light over the elevator dinged on. "Not really. Busy with work."

"Life is more than work." They stepped into the elevator, and the doors shut behind them.

Desmond watched the numbers light up near the ceiling. "And you, Archer? If you weren't working, where would you be?"

"Going out and getting drunk with friends," she retorted immediately.

He almost smiled. "Really?"

She lifted one shoulder. "No. Not really. Used to. My sister and I used to tear up the town. After she died, it kind of killed my partying mood. I've got Camille and Samara at work. And Gemma. But I'm not one for lots of friends." Her voice was calm, but Desmond by now knew her well enough to hear the careful carelessness of the words. He knew it because he'd perfected his version of it over the years.

"I didn't know. Older or younger?"

"Older."

"I'm sorry."

"Me too."

Desmond got to his door, unlocking it and stepping aside as Remi went in first, the routine now second nature. She checked all the rooms, then met him back in the living room. He stood at his desk facing a pile of papers that mocked his silence.

"All right. See you bright and early," Remi said, giving him a half-hearted salute.

"Wait," he said, the word dragged out of him before he could reconsider it for the eighth time.

She immediately stopped, one word from him and he had her undivided, and significant, attention. It made his breath catch for a moment, until he reminded himself that this was just a job to her, and refocused. "These are for you."

He put his hand on top of the papers that had been slowly accumulating over the week. First, it was a pretense, in case she asked, then it became a habit, to make extra copies of his cases. Then they sat on his desk, waiting for him to get over his arrogance.

Brow arched, she approached, opening the first folder, skimming over the first few pages. "Case files?"

He turned away, grabbing a small envelope from his bag. "Obviously. And this." He put it on top of the folders and opened up his bag, pulling out the work he'd brought home.

"What is it?" she asked, holding up the envelope.

Desmond didn't look up. "A check. Continuation of services."

She grinned, shoving it into her pocket. "I knew you liked me."

He shook his head, unable to keep the corner of his mouth from tilting up. "I like being not dead."

"Tomato, potato."

"That's for two weeks," he added. "If you catch him before then, I want a refund."

"We'll see about that," she laughed, grabbing the files under one arm.

She was almost to the door when he spoke. "The funeral is on Saturday. You don't need to—"

Remi turned. "I do need to. But even if I didn't, I'd be there, Des."

He blinked a bit at the nickname, but she smiled, waving her free hand. "See you in the morning. Lock up behind me."

"Always do," he said, trailing behind her.

Remi grinned. "Hey, gotta keep reminding you. You're getting on in years, you know."

He rolled his eyes, locking the door behind her, and speaking loudly enough that she heard through the wood. "You're a pain, sweetheart."

The surprised laughter echoed through the door, and Desmond listened to it fade, a smile on his face.

****

Saturday dawned cold and gray, appropriate for the events to come.

Desmond took care in selecting his clothes. He had to look the part of a mourning son, if only for Ashley's benefit. As he buttoned up the shirt, he caught a

41

glimpse of the white marks on his chest in the mirror. The black fabric covered them up, but only three people knew they were there.

Now, only two.

His phone buzzed, with a text from Remi saying she was five minutes out. Desmond went without the briefcase this time, taking a messenger bag with the documents for the cemetery and paperwork to deal with the death certificate. Another glance in the mirror assured him he looked the part.

He unnecessarily straightened the tie, then took the stairs down. On the last flight Remi texted she was here. Pushing through the door, he recognized the car on the sidewalk as the one she'd driven him home in that first night.

"Hey."

He turned, his greeting never making it past his lips. Gone were the jeans and boots, replaced with a modest black dress and black heels. Gone was the leather jacket, replaced with a tailored coat. But most surprisingly, gone was the loose hair. Instead, the blonde locks were pulled back up into a simple bun at the base of her neck.

Desmond cleared his throat. "You clean up nice."

She gave him a faint smile. "Was that a compliment?"

"An observation."

She grinned. "Yeah, sure, whatever you say." She opened the passenger door for him, shut it, and walked around to the driver's seat. She checked the street, then pulled out onto the road as he stared out the window.

Today would be rough only in that he was worried about Ashley and some of the other guests. He didn't care that his father was dead. He'd been dead to him since the day he was put behind bars. It was the only case Desmond had ever lost as a defense attorney before he switched to the prosecution side of things. No one blamed him, as his father had been guilty, but it was the one case he'd lost. If he could even call it that.

Remi cleared her throat, clearly wanting his attention. He turned back to her, catching her gaze as it darted toward him, then back to the street. "I know you're gonna hate hearing this, but it's gotta be said. I know this isn't something we can skip, but I'd really rather we could, 'cause this whole thing smells like a setup. Open area, no security, no checking of persons or weapons before approach. Kind of my nightmare. Could just be my paranoia, but..." She shrugged, glancing at him. "I'm gonna need you to stay by my side the whole time. If I say stop, you stop. If I say run, you book it. Understand?"

Desmond looked at her again, ignoring the drastic change in appearance and noticing a few new things. The lines at her mouth, the tight grip on the steering wheel, the gun under her coat.

"Understood," he said quietly, looking back at the road.

He caught her nod at the edge of his vision, but her gaze continued to stray back as she wove between the light traffic.

"What?" he eventually sighed.

"Ashley. Does she know?" she asked quietly.

"I haven't said anything about the stalker, but she knows that you're protection—"

"No. Sorry. I mean, does she know what your father did to you?"

He didn't ask her what she meant. Didn't even ask how she knew. Both answers were too obvious—the file on him, the scars she saw that first night.

He stared straight ahead. "I don't know. We've never discussed it. I've never asked."

She glanced over at him as she slowed to a stop at a red light. "Why?"

"My sister worshipped our father," he said, consciously keeping his hands relaxed. "If I tell her and she didn't know, I would be taking away something precious to her. If I tell her, and she already knew…" He trailed off.

Remi exhaled quietly. "Right. Shit."

"Yeah."

****

Everett Graves, for the low-level stain he cast upon the world, garnered an interesting group of mourners. Despite the simple graveside service, it was crowded with guests. Ashley and Rick were obvious. Low-tiered members of some of the local gangs, were not entirely surprising. The cops were a twist.

But the poisoned cherry on Remi's day was the sight of James Delaney.

James fucking Delaney. Brilliant but psychotic, discredited scientist. The current head of the Blackheart Gang. Horrifying.

She kept her focus on Delaney and his cronies, the only ones who made no secret they were openly carrying. Keeping close to Desmond's side, she angled herself to stay between him and Delaney as they approached the plot. "What the hell did he have in common with your father?" she hissed at Desmond.

He didn't flinch as he looked up. "Me."

Remi didn't get a chance to ask anything else as they got to the gravesite. Everyone sported appropriate mourning attire, even Rick had found a dark suit. The priest stood at the headstone, talking quietly with Ashley. Remi noted her red-rimmed eyes and tried to remind herself that whatever piece of garbage Everett was, he'd been Ashley and Desmond's father.

Desmond stood near the head of Everett's plot, Remi positioned herself at his shoulder. She kept her head on a swivel, looking at every newcomer who approached to express condolences.

Her skin started to itch—too many were armed, too many were dangerous. She couldn't protect Desmond here. Not effectively. They had to leave—

"My father," Ashley began, creating a hush over the crowd, "was a strong, opinionated man. He didn't get along with everyone. But those who mattered knew him." She nodded at the crowd, cops and crooks returning the gesture. "He was the best man I've ever known."

Only because Remi was still looking around at the crowd did she see Desmond's jaw jump slightly. She listened with half an ear as Ashley continued to discuss the imagined good qualities of her father. She seemed completely honest though, and Remi wondered what it was like to be that ignorant about someone, especially someone like Everett.

Though, to be fair, people were that ignorant about her, too.

Remi caught the gaze of Delaney from across the grave. He looked her up and down, marking the gun at her hip and missing the knife at her thigh. Delaney slowly lifted his eyes back up to hers and winked.

It took everything in her not to flip him off. A warm hand pressed against her back, and Remi glanced down to see Desmond's arm reaching around her, casually demonstrating a connection. He didn't look at her, but it was the first conscious gesture he'd made toward her. His palm was warm where he touched her, and she could feel it through her coat and shirt. She resisted the urge to lean into it, cutting her eyes up at Desmond instead.

He was looking at his sister, but as Remi looked back, Delaney was staring at Desmond, surprise written all over his face.

Ashley seemed to be wrapping up. "Dad always said that when you back someone into a corner, when you take away their safety nets, they'll show you who you really are. He showed that he would do whatever it takes."

Desmond's scoff was nearly silent, and Remi almost missed it, but the echo passed through his hand and against her back.

"I'll miss him," Ashley choked, stepping away from the headstone and back to Desmond. She reached out to him, and Desmond immediately extended his hand to her. "Do you want to say something?" she asked.

It was clear he wanted to say no, and Remi would have given anything to keep him from having to speak for his father, but Ashley's face was pleading, insistence driven by the ignorance Remi wasn't lucky enough to have.

His hand dropped from Remi's back but she grabbed it, almost on instinct. "Des," she said quietly, unsure if it was her place, but unable to remain silent.

"It's fine." He pulled his hand from hers and strode past her to the head of the coffin.

Remi felt Ashley's eyes on her but didn't turn away from Desmond.

"My father..." Desmond trailed off, staring at the coffin, before clearing his throat. "My father taught me a lot of hard lessons about life." His voice was steady, each word carefully considered before escaping his mouth, falling with a steady honesty, even though Remi knew he wasn't telling the whole truth. "I wouldn't be the man I am if not for him. Even though he's gone, he left a lot to remember him by, and I'll carry it with me until I see him again." He stared at the coffin for a long, silent moment, before stepping away and returning to Remi's side. He didn't replace his hand.

Her fists were clenched in the pockets of her coat, and she kept her eyes straight forward as a few other people spoke over this piece of trash. Did no one else know? Or did none of them care? Remi scanned the crowd, looking for those who might know about the scars on Desmond's torso. Someone had to have known, yet no one did anything. Death was too good for Everett Graves.

Finally, Ashley picked up a handful of dirt and threw it down upon the coffin. Desmond did the same, though with a hesitation. The damp earth thudded against the wooden coffin, echoing in the air.

With that, the crowd began to disperse. Desmond let out a quiet exhale and turned to face Remi. "A few goodbyes, then we're good to leave," he murmured.

Remi nodded, not trusting herself to open her mouth just yet. Desmond walked over to Ashley and Rick, the three of them alone by the headstone. Remi kept her eyes on the crowd, staying between them and any who went to approach them. Several did, though they had to walk by Remi first. She gauged them all, letting them pass one at a time. That is, until Delaney began approaching.

She stepped in his way, but he stopped, unperturbed, and addressed her. "Good afternoon," he said. "I didn't realize Desi would be bringing a date."

"It's Desmond. And I didn't realize you'd be crawling out of your lair to attend the funeral of an errand boy," Remi retorted.

Delaney smiled, the thin gesture not reaching his eyes. "Bold words for such a small woman. You are Remi Archer, correct?"

She just arched her brow. He'd be stupid if he couldn't identify someone like her. People like him didn't walk into a new place without knowing everyone else in the area. It's something they had in common.

"I've heard of you," he said, ignoring her lack of response. "But perhaps some of that was exaggerated. Seeing you now, I doubt that you are capable of half of the stories." He smiled at the man next to him, big, bulky, and obviously the muscle. Remi had met dozens of men who referred to themselves as the "muscle." Muscle didn't equal skill.

She imitated his smile. "Doubt? Or hope?"

He merely smiled wider.

"Nonetheless," she said, rolling her eyes, "you could always ask my old pal, Aldous Timms," naming a high-level drug dealer she'd helped to arrest. "Or Yancy Jones," she added, remembering he'd been a heavy hitter for the Blackhearts before trying to make it on his own. He hadn't lasted long, and she'd sent him to prison with several fewer fingers. "I'd be happy to describe our last meeting in detail."

A flicker of recognition indicated he knew exactly what Remi was referring to, and it made her warm inside to see fear on his creepy face. "Out of respect for my close friend," Delaney said, leaning in, "I won't punish you for your insolence."

Remi's brow arched and she took a step forward, getting uncomfortably close, and grinning up at him. "I would love to see you try."

"Archer."

She didn't look away as Des returned to her side.

"Desi." Delaney's voice was almost a croon. "So wonderful to see you. Though one wishes it wasn't under such unfortunate circumstances."

"Yeah," he said, voice cool. "Unfortunate there's one less person in the world who shares your favorite pastimes."

"If you think I don't have many who indulge my hobbies, you're mistaken," Delaney said, the smile on his face cruel.

It clicked now, what Desmond had meant earlier. The scars, what his father had done—he hadn't been the only one to inflict them—

Her anger burned in his fingertips, but she saw Desmond's chin go up, and his fists clenched, so Remi did what she was paid to do. "Yeah, Des," she said casually. "It's amazing what people will do for a quick buck, I'm sure this guy can get all kinds of people to shit on him for fun."

Delaney had probably been threatened by dozens and dozens of people. Horrible, desperate things hurled at him by hundreds of people.

But she was willing to bet no one had ever said anything like *that*.

Mouth agape, Delaney couldn't come up with any vaguely threatening line to say. Even Desmond was staring at her, but his eyes were dancing, amazed and annoyed in almost equal measures.

"Come on," Remi said, turning her back on Delaney. "This place smells like a sewer."

Desmond nodded at Delaney, then fell into step with her. Despite her power move, Remi remained tense, blocking Desmond as best she could and her hand hovering over her waist until they were safely ensconced in the car. Only then did Remi let her head lean back on the headrest and let out a long sigh

Desmond ran his hand over his face, covering his mouth as he stared at her.

"What?" she asked.

"You just insulted the head of the Blackheart Gang. You suggested—"

"No. I stated."

Both hands went up to cover his face. "Are you clinically insane?"

"Jury's out. What do you think, prosecutor?"

A strange sound came from between his fingers, and Remi sat up, leaning towards him. "Are you *laughing*, Graves?"

He dropped his hands, the smile on his face so unexpected today of all days. Remi couldn't help but smile back at him. "You insulted James Delaney," he repeated, the grin on his face making it clear he didn't mind all that much.

"Two seconds earlier, I threatened him, too," Remi added, turning on the car.

"Definitely insane," he muttered, sitting back.

Remi pulled out onto the street and hesitated at the light. Her adrenaline was thrumming beneath her skin, the anger not fading completely. Reaching a decision, she asked, "You have any plans today?"

He glanced at her out of the corner of his eye. "What did you have in mind?"

Chapter Four

Exceptional Security was housed in an impressively modern building. All chrome and metal, it was the epitome of high class, even though it was located in the warehouse district. Tall glass windows lined the front lobby, where sat a petite brunette at a massive desk with a cavalcade of security measures. Following closely on Remi's heels, both hands in his coat pockets, Desmond took it all in with one glance.

"Miss Archer," said the woman, standing up behind the desk. "You look lovely."

"Don't get used to it." Remi glanced over her shoulder at him. "Gemma, meet Desmond Graves. Graves, this is Gemma Hart, the brains around here. If it weren't for her, someone would've shot our boss a long time ago."

"It undoubtedly would have been you," Gemma retorted, holding out her hand for Desmond to shake.

He did, feeling mildly bemused at the exchange. "Pleasure."

Gemma's smile was a little too wicked for him to believe that she was all that prim and proper, despite her professional demeanor. "It's a pleasure to meet you, Mr. Graves. I've heard quite a bit about you."

"Is that so?" he said, glancing at Remi.

She rolled her eyes and typed in something on the computer.

"So this is where you security types work?"

"Miss Archer has her office and apartment here, though her work may take her many places," Gemma answered.

Desmond's eyes briefly flickered between Gemma and Remi; he settled on answering with a simple nod. So she hadn't just brought him to her place of work, it was also her home.

Interesting.

"Thanks, Gemma," Remi said, brow arched in annoyance.

The woman smiled as if she didn't know what she'd revealed, then returned to her desk and started clicking a few buttons. She returned to them with a card on a lanyard and passed it to Desmond. "This will give you access to all unrestricted areas of the base. Enjoy your stay."

Desmond hung the lanyard around his neck, then he gestured to Remi, who had crossed her arms. "Lead the way."

She did, and Desmond followed, ignoring the feel of Gemma's gaze on his back. Pushing her way through a set of overly tall glass doors, Remi led the way upstairs. "If you don't mind, I'm gonna change first."

"I don't mind," he said, still looking around.

For a security building, it was startlingly open and airy. He'd imagined it briefly as a closed-off space, with close metal walls and too many grates. Though the walls were still metal, it was manageable. More importantly, it was a distraction from the day, and that was all he was looking for right now.

She turned left at the top of the stairs, nodding to a woman in the first room. "Hey, Cam."

"Good afternoon, Remi. And you must be Desmond Graves."

The beautiful young woman moved with a grace that Desmond had never before seen on a human. He'd heard about Camille Juma from Rick, and seen a few photos, but they didn't do her justice. She smiled, her lips curling up as she nodded her head at Desmond, not attempting to shake his hand. "I've heard so much about you, both from Remi and Rick."

"Mind entertaining him for a minute?" Remi asked. "I need to get out of this dress before I throw a fit."

Camille smiled, amusement lacing her voice as she turned back to Desmond. "Remi can play any part she'd like, but when she gets back here, all illusions are shattered." She gestured for him to follow her into the room. He stopped just inside the threshold and leaned on the door, taking it in.

Camille's bedroom was bright and airy, the window uncovered and small trinkets lining the sill. Her sheets were a mess of different colors and fabrics, bright yellows and greens, blues and oranges giving some color to the monotone room. Everything seemed to be in its place, a sense of order and tidiness clear in the small space.

The knives on the nightstand gave him pause, but not enough for him to comment.

"How are you enjoying working with Remi?" Camille asked, leaning against a wooden desk on the opposite side of the room.

"When one isn't given a choice, can it really be termed 'working with'?" he responded.

"True. I am sorry for the circumstances." Camille turned, picking up a file from her desk and rifling through it. "Has there been any headway in the case?"

"Not that she's told me."

"Then there hasn't been headway. Remi is many things, but she would never keep you in the dark about your safety."

Desmond found that he agreed with her. "I know."

Camille placed the file down. "Despite her being my friend, Remi can be a little difficult. I hope she hasn't been making your life too challenging."

"Only when she's nearby."

Her laughter was honest and full, and Desmond smiled despite his comment. Still, he felt he had to add, "Though we've been making it work."

"I'm happy to hear it. She's an amazing agent, but I feel that sometimes she allows her job to become her life. I'm glad she's getting out more."

"In case you forgot, I am a job."

Camille just smiled, her response lost as Remi returned. She was back to the same old Remi, in her tank top, jeans, and boots, but he noticed she wasn't wearing her jacket this time.

"Thanks," she said to Camille.

"Of course. It was a pleasure to meet you in person, Desmond."

"And you."

Camille smiled as they left.

Desmond fell back into place beside Remi, noticing the bag she held in one hand. He held his questions, though, and followed Remi down the hall to a completely separate staircase. It led down two landings, which had to be below ground, and she pushed open the heavy wooden door at the bottom.

As Desmond stepped through, he managed to keep

his mouth closed, but his brows shot up. The whole floor, which was at least as large as the previous two combined, was a massive gym and training center. Exercise equipment lined the wall, punching bags hanging from multiple points behind them. Just to the left of the center was a boxing ring, with the gloves neatly arranged around it. Lining the whole right wall, and where Remi led him, was a significant gun range.

"Seems like a large place for just you and Camille," Desmond finally said.

Remi grinned at him over her shoulder. "Fishing for info?" She didn't wait for a response and continued anyway, heading into the gun range and grabbing two headphones. "There're three agents now, the ones who go out and protect people. A couple we're working with may join. Me, Cam, and Samara—Samara Latif—are the senior agents. Aiden used to be part of it, but he left after a couple of years to take care of his mother. Alec Singh is technically a client, but he's been hanging around here more than necessary and making changes to some of our tech for free. He seems to be enjoying himself, so he might stay on."

She grabbed a paper target from a stack and hung it up on their lane. "Farid Nassar was a client until three days ago, and we haven't gotten rid of him. He's good at research, so no one really minds. And Rick likes to come here to blow off some steam."

"Are you trying to steal my investigator?" he asked, leaning against the partition between rows.

She smiled that little smirk of hers that made his shoulders relax automatically. "Our boss is Thomas Jones, he's not down here all that often, though. And Gemma is all about the paperwork. So I usually have this place mostly to myself." She opened up her bag, pulled out several metal pieces, then put them all together until she held a fully formed weapon.

"This holds seven rounds," she said, holding it out to him and gesturing as she spoke. "Safety's on the side. Leave it on unless you want to shoot something. Always two hands, unless you're an assassin or a terminator, because the kickback might knock your teeth out otherwise. Aim for center mass—biggest target and statistically more likely payout. Before you shoot, exhale, then squeeze, don't pull."

She handed him a set of headphones, but he didn't put them on just yet.

"And we're doing this, why?" he asked.

"Helping to blow off some steam. Giving you a target to shoot at, since you can't shoot anything else that's been bugging you. Teaching you something." Then shrugged and mirrored his position on the opposite side. "Trying to get your mind off things."

He eyed her speculatively, trying to figure out what was different. Because something was off. Then his gaze trailed down, noting the marks on her arms, the scars that crisscrossed her skin in a variety of patterns. She was comfortable here. Comfortable enough to not need her jacket as a shield.

Comfortable enough with him.

Figuring he'd give it a try, he finally nodded and stepped up. Remi reached for the gun, but he held out his hand. "No, if we're doing this, I'm going first."

"Confident?"

"Not in the slightest. There's just no way I'm going after you."

She smirked. "I am amazing."

"Wasn't the word I was thinking of," he muttered, getting a laugh in response.

"All right, hotshot," she said, putting her headphones on. "Have at it."

She pressed a button, and the target zoomed back down the lane.

Desmond put on the headphones and stepped up, picking up the gun on the counter. It was heavier than he'd anticipated, denser. He'd held a few guns in his life but never shot anything.

He aimed at the target with both hands and fired. It did rocket in his hands, but he controlled it and placed the gun back down. He slid his headphones down around his neck as Remi took hers off.

"Not bad," she commented.

It clipped the edge of the target, almost not counting as a hit, but at least he'd hit the paper. He felt proud of himself. Then Remi stepped up, gesturing for him to put on his headphones again. She picked the gun up one-handed and fired three quick shots. All three holes clustered in the center. When she brought the target back up, he saw they were so close the holes connected.

The smell of gun smoke was strong, but he was familiar enough with it not to wrinkle his nose. Remi was looking at him, so he said, "Thought you said two hands."

"Unless," she reminded him, taking down the target and replacing it with a new one.

He recalled the specifics of her statement and hid his frown. "I knew you weren't human."

With a laugh, she sent the target back. She turned to him. "Wanna go again?"

Part of him did, but he could gain something else here. A few questions that needed answers, and he'd always had an insatiable curiosity. He weighed his options for a moment, knowing what he'd give up in return, and spoke anyway. "How about we make this a little more interesting?"

She cocked a brow, leaning against the partition behind her. "Strip shooting never turns out well, I warn you."

He smiled. "Not what I had in mind."

"Then do tell. I can shoot circles around you."

Desmond resisted the urge to roll his eyes. "That's my point. I can't outshoot you—"

"Obviously."

"So there's no point in me trying. However, I can improve, which I assume is part of the goal of this little venture?"

She shrugged, keeping her eyes on him.

"If I can improve on my shot, you have to answer a question honestly—"

That got her to react. She pushed away from the wall, the frown that had been absent since they left the cemetery returning in full. "Wait, I've been honest with you about *everything*."

"—about you," he finished, stepping forward to pacify her. He knew she was telling the truth about everything he'd asked. It was what he hadn't asked yet.

That made the anger fade, replacing it with a cautious, skeptical stare. "Why?"

"Curiosity."

"Dangerous waters, prosecutor," she said, but the frown faded. Desmond felt his shoulders relax as her smile returned, hating the idea of making her upset. A long way from a week ago.

"What do I get out of this?" she asked.

"If you make whatever shot I say, you get to ask me something."

"Who says there's anything I want to know?"

He smiled, the confidence he felt in the courtroom coming to play here. He knew this game. "Call it intuition."

"All right. I'll bite. Let's go."

Desmond took his time this second time around. He reviewed what Remi had said, aimed, exhaled, and squeezed. The bullet hole still wasn't center, but it was closer than before.

"Fast learner," she said, as he removed his headphones. "Guess you get a question." She crossed her arms, her mouth still turned up in a smile, but he could see some concern in her eyes.

He thought for a moment, sorting through his curiosities. He decided. "That first night. What did you mean when you said you know how to deal with monsters?"

Remi didn't flinch. "Exactly what I said. I've got experience."

"How so?"

"Sounds like two questions."

"Honesty means the entire truth," he countered.

She turned to the counter, avoiding his eyes for the first time since they'd met. "I am one."

****

Remi felt Desmond's eyes on her as she stood in front of the counter, her hand resting next to the gun. She let the silence linger for a moment, knowing he would wait for her to answer. It wasn't that she didn't know what to say. it was that she did but was unsure if he wanted to hear it.

Well, he'd asked for honesty. He was about to fucking regret that.

"I was a mercenary," she said, staring at the counter. The top was chipped and she picked at the mark. "After my few years in the military, I left. I hated fighting people who didn't deserve to die. I wanted to go after the ones who'd sent them there in the first place. So, I fell in with a…group, of sorts. They trained me, and I worked for them. I killed people for them. Mostly terrible people, too powerful to reach by any legal means. But sometimes, they seemed like decent folks. I told myself I was doing the right thing."

She recalled the little girl who'd seen her covered in her father's blood. Her last job.

"Then, after a bad job, I realized I wasn't. So I ran. Struggled. Got into trouble, until Thomas picked me up one day. He knew every messed-up detail about me and my past and asked if I wanted to make amends." She recalled that with painful clarity. How he'd read out her long, long list of mistakes and offered her a chance to do something good.

"I thought it would be impossible, that I'd never make up for the shit I'd done. I'm the best because I know how monsters think. They do exactly what I did. Sometimes I still think that it'll never be enough, that I've still taken more than I can save." Her voice had quieted, not of a conscious decision. She shook it off and shrugged. "But, what the hell, this pays better, and I sleep a little easier at night, so it's worth it."

She picked at the counter again, not wanting to look at him. Would he hightail it out of here, or look at her like she was a monster? Would he ask for someone else? It was harder than she expected, facing him. Despite how this started, she enjoyed his company. So much so that she brought him here. And if he hated her, or feared her, or thought she was—

"The heart."

She frowned, lifting her eyes to his. Desmond was staring at her with mix of emotions on his face, but she couldn't parse it. He turned away, looking down the lane. "Your shot. Two through the heart."

Hesitating, Remi didn't reach for the weapon until he looked back down at her. The corner of his mouth lifted as drawled, "What's the matter, terminator? Scared you can't make it?"

The tension within her dissipated with the new moniker. She grinned as she picked up the piece. "Get ready to spill."

They both put on their headphones. She aimed and fired twice without much focus. She pressed the button to drag it back to them, seeing the single hole in the heart, where her two bullets had entered.

Desmond shook his head, scoffing. "Impressive."

"I know."

He was holding himself a little straighter, his arms crossing over his chest. "It's time for me to pay up."

Remi kept her eyes low as she reloaded the gun, recognizing his tells of discomfort. One thing about him had been niggling at her over the past week. She wasn't going to pass up the opportunity to get some answers. She glanced up at him. "So, does anyone else know you threw your dad's case?"

His arms unfolded, and his brow went up, but he didn't say anything.

"Come on," she said, canting her head at him. "Hotshot lawyer like you only loses one case in his entire career, and it's his father's? If you think I didn't go over that case with a fine-tooth comb, especially knowing what kind of man he was, you're wrong."

"How'd you know?" he said, admitting without saying it. He took off the headphones, passing them between his fingers.

"You brought up the cigarettes. Set him right up for the prosecution, and they knocked him down. It was poetic."

Desmond's smile was unlike anything she had ever seen before. It was so full of dark satisfaction that he'd brought down the man who'd abused him. It was also kind of hot.

"You ever think about going into law, Archer? You've got a talent."

"And wear boring suits every day? No, thanks."

Desmond's smile vanished as he spoke. "I knew he was guilty. He made me represent him anyway. I'd never lost a case before because my clients were always innocent. But Everett..." He shook his head. "He told me that he bought the cigarettes at the convenience store where he shot the victim, Edwards. He had a friend put on his shirt and hat since the two of them looked similar. Then his friend bought a forty and a pack of cigarettes an hour's drive away with his credit card."

"But it was the wrong brand."

"My father only ever had loyalty to two things—himself and his smokes. I dropped the hint, and the prosecution did the rest. The next day, I quit being a defense attorney. I didn't want to be behind the ball. I didn't want to defend the victims, I wanted to go after the people who hurt them."

Remi shook her head, impressed at his audacity. He gave up his reputation, and risked his entire career, to take down his father. Desmond Graves was unbelievable. A modern-day hero, smart, clever, sarcastic as hell, handsome—

Wait, what?

Desmond stilled, his eyes going distant and the headphones hanging limp in his hand.

She pushed aside wayward, inappropriate, and un-fucking-helpful thoughts. "Des?"

"The last conversation I had with him, Everett. It was a year ago, so I didn't...but he said—"

"Hey," she said, stepping up to him and placing her hand on his arm. "Full sentences."

"My father suspected I threw his case, but he couldn't prove it. I never said anything, and no one else had a clue, but Everett. I met with him a year ago, about Ashley's nonexistent trust." Desmond looked down at her. "He said he knew I threw the case. And he said I'd be sorry. If I cared so much about my career and so little for my family, that I would lose everything. And the notes—"

Stop or you'll be sorry.

Do you care about your career more than your life?

Drop the case or lose everything.

She ignored the chills that appeared, recalling the letters. She approached the wall and jammed her hand onto a button. "Gemma!"

Gemma's voice echoed throughout the room, punctuated with the briefest sigh. "Yes, Miss Archer?"

"I need everything you've got on Everett Graves." She unloaded the gun and took it apart, still talking. "Former gangs he ran with, cellmates, his dealers, his front men, his dentist, everyone."

"Of course, but Everett Graves died the other day. Why are we investigating him?"

She shut the gun case with a loud snap. "Because as of this moment, he's my number one suspect."

****

They left the building shortly after that, neither of them up for playing a game in the face of the revelation. Gemma was no longer smiling as they passed through the lobby. She gave a curt nod to Remi as she spoke on the phone. Desmond thought he saw the logo of the police database, but Remi never stopped long enough for him to check. They returned to the car, Remi's usual checks taking a little longer.

The ride was silent. Desmond sat against the door, enjoying the numbness that came with the revelation. It made sense. Everett had made his life a living hell while he was alive, and younger Desmond had thought he was a demon. It only made sense he'd be able to continue from beyond the grave. He closed his eyes and rested his head against the headrest.

Despite how much he hated his father, Desmond couldn't ignore a sense of disappointment. He knew what kind of man his father was. But at the same time, hurt still sprouted in his chest. Hurt that his father had yet again shown he didn't care for him. Disappointment that yet again, his father didn't act as a father should. The guilt was still there for Desmond, even after years of knowing that he had been the victim.

He ran his hand along his arm, to the first scar he

could remember getting. It was a circular burn mark, from the very cigarettes which had gotten Everett imprisoned. He couldn't feel it through the shirt and jacket, but he knew it was there. He still felt guilty. Like it had been something he'd done or didn't do. That he could've changed what happened. Logically, he knew he was a kid when it started. Kids don't deserve that. Not even him. He inhaled and closed his eyes, his chest feeling too tight.

"You doing all right?" Remi's voice was soft as she stopped at a red light. "If there's anything—"

"Don't." The revving of the engine almost drowned out his words. "Don't do that."

"Do what?"

"Don't be nice to me because of this."

Teachers who'd noticed his limp, or lovers who'd seen his scars, had pitied him. Doctors pitied him the few times he'd been in bad enough shape to need them. Those looks left a film over his skin and an insurmountable barrier to the relationship. He'd had enough pity to last a lifetime, and he didn't want it— couldn't handle it—from Remi.

A beat of silence followed before she exploded. "You want to be a martyr, huh? Well, you're gonna have to suck it up, old man. Dead or not, I'm tearing your father's legacy down. So you're gonna have to find a new aspect of your shitty childhood to be dramatic about. That better?"

Not looking at him, she reached across the seat and covered his hand with hers. Desmond stared at that connection, his thoughts tangling in his head.

Remi walked with him to his door, a little more tense than usual, but doing a decent job of hiding it. But

Desmond could tell with how she walked a little farther from him to give herself a better range of movement. Her footsteps were silent; she kept her responses short.

She checked the apartment while he took off his coat and placed his bag on the counter. He turned on a light in the kitchen but left the rest of them off. It was only seven, but he was feeling the effects of the day and decided he would head to bed early. Remi met him in the kitchen, giving him a nod to show everything was clear. He said nothing as he followed her down the short hallway to the door. It was dark, making the shadows seem longer.

"All set, I'll talk to you in the morning," she said, grabbing the handle. "Try not to get up too early, I get bitchy when people wake me up on the weekends."

"How could I tell the difference?"

She grinned and turned to go. "Goodnight, hotshot."

"Remi?"

She paused in the door, both of them a little startled he used her first name.

"Thank you."

"Careful," she teased, a grin on her face. "It sounds like you like having me around."

"God forbid."

Despite his words, he knew it was too late for that. He liked having her around. He liked her comments and wit. And though he'd never wanted a stalker, it wasn't so bad if someone like Remi was looking out for him. In fact, he would even say that he liked her.

Without warning, Remi leaned in and hugged him. Her arms slid around his waist, and her head tucked under his chin. He didn't see it coming, which he'd later argue was the only reason he didn't try to avoid it, though it was a lie.

In the dark, after such a miserable day, he'd admit that it felt nice. As much as he appreciated the bluntness, this was necessary. He hesitated a moment, then his arm came up and wrapped around her, pulling her tighter against him. His lips pressed against her hair, and her arms squeezed tighter. She felt so warm beneath the cool leather, a flame turned human. The warmth slid into his chest and stayed there.

Resting her cheek on his chest, she repeated her earlier promise. "You need anything, I'm there."

"Thank you," he said again, this time softer.

With a final gentle squeeze, Remi released him with a wink. "Lock up—"

He rolled his eyes. "I know."

She waggled her fingers at him. "Goodnight."

He shut the door behind her, clicking the lock as loudly as he could. Then he walked to the window, staring down at the street. He couldn't see the car from here, but he was able to catch the taillights as she pulled out into the street.

He pulled out his phone and then put it down. Irritated with himself, he picked it up and sent a message before he reconsidered.

—Goodnight.—

He put it back down on the counter as he unpacked his bag. He emptied all the papers he'd collected and signed throughout the day. Two manilla envelopes hit the table, and he opened them to file the papers away.

One contained his father's death certificate. He put that with the papers he had to bring to work on Monday. He then bent the pegs back on the other envelope and reached in—

His phone buzzed, revealing that Remi had sent him back a smiley face and a note.

—Night, Des. See you tomorrow.—

He was still smiling when he lifted the papers from the folder. The smile vanished and his breath halted as he saw the photograph in his hands.

Chapter Five

When she arrived at Exceptional Security, Remi grabbed everyone and dragged them to the conference room. She needed to find a connection between Everett and the threats. Even if that meant she had to comb through all Desmond's active cases and Delaney's criminal history.

Which is why, when they'd found nothing in the first three hours, she'd become pissed off. She retreated to the gym, working her frustration into the mat. Dragging herself out of there, she crashed for an hour. Afterward, she returned to the conference room, determined not to leave again until they found something.

"I think I got something," Farid Nassar spoke up from between a pile of court documents and a box full of Chinese food.

It was after two A.M., but no one complained. A few had begged off for a few hours of sleep before returning, but they were all here to help. She looked up from the laptop she was on, blinked a couple of times, and focused on the historian. "What have you got?"

"Might be nothing, but Sam Landon is one of his cases, right?"

"Yes." Days ago she'd memorized the extensive list of Graves's current cases. "He's up on charges first-degree murder. Trial starts this week. Why?"

"Mr. Landon was in the same prison as Everett Graves—at the same time. Just for two months at the beginning of Graves's term, and they didn't share a cell. So, it may be nothing. But my gut says it's something."

Remi grabbed Landon's file, distributing copies to everyone in the room. "Find the connection."

An hour later, Thomas was the one to strike gold. "Have any of you ever heard of Yancy Jones?"

Remi frowned. She remembered him. Real well.

"He ran with a crowd called the Blackheart Gang until Delaney took over," Thomas murmured. "Mr. Jones attempted to start a new gang until Miss Archer took him down." Looking over Thomas's shoulder, Gemma nodded in agreement.

Damn.

"And Landon was working for Yancy when Delaney came in."

Shit.

"Landon worked for Delaney for two months before his first arrest. It was such a short period, it was never brought up in his cases, but this article here confirms it." He handed it over to Remi.

Skimming it, Remi saw everything corroborated on the paper. Landon was in the Blackheart Gang and stayed after Delaney took over. After that, he went to prison, where he ran into Everett, who had his own arrangement with Delaney.

"He got out of prison and seemed to fall right back in with the Blackheart Gang, before his most recent arrest." Thomas took the article back. "I don't have a connection to Graves, yet, other than he's the lawyer prosecuting him, but—"

"There's a connection," Remi said. "Everett and Delaney had this neat little club where they abused kids." No one spoke after that until Remi looked up. "What did Landon do for Jones?"

"Hitman."

Dammit.

"Okay," said Remi, raising her voice, though no one else was speaking. "Working theory: Delaney is going after Graves to make him drop the case on his cleaner. The timing makes sense, and there's a connection between Delaney and Everett. That matches our theory on the notes. Bonus points, the guy is trying to get back at Graves on Everett's behalf. He lost his partner, so he's getting even. Find out who's in the gang as of today and get me everything you've got."

Camille pulled Remi aside as the rest of them went back to work. "You need to get some sleep."

"I'm fine, I can—"

"You have to be at Mr. Graves's side all day and review all his cases as well. You need to rest. It's going to take us some time to get all that information. We've got this."

The look on her face made it clear that she wouldn't take no as an answer. Remi had faced off against Camille in the gym too often not to appreciate the implied threat. "Fine. But if you find something—"

"We'll put it in a file for when you wake up. Get some sleep."

Remi trudged off to bed, feeling Camille's glare at her back until she was out of sight.

Her room was on the end of the hall she led Desmond to yesterday and had only one small window. She'd chosen it for that reason; there were fewer entrances. When she'd first moved in, she'd kept the room as sparse as possible. Despite Thomas's suggestion that she could use the job to ease her conscience, she'd waited for any excuse to leave.

Now, pictures hung on the closet doors and around the windowsill. Her sister's and father's smiles, Camille and Samara, even several of her and Aiden before he left. Everyone who mattered and believed that she could be more. The closet was overflowing with her clothes. Knives glinted beneath half-finished books and incomplete reports for Thomas.

Plugging in her phone, Remi turned the volume up all the way. She glanced once more at the message from Desmond, smiled, and fell asleep.

When she woke up at six, the only new thing in the digital file her team had created was a list of names. None were familiar to her, so she put it aside for now and checked on Desmond. His tracker had him in his penthouse, so she sent him a text.

—I'm up. Let me know when you're awake and ready for company. We've got some shit to sort through.—

It was still early, so she went down and spent an hour in the gym, then took a shower. On the way to the conference room, she grabbed a bagel from the kitchen on the second floor. It was small, but energy-efficient and stocked with their favorites. Gemma ordered the groceries for them, never forgetting Samara's tea or Remi's bagels. After checking with Camille, who had nothing new to report, Remi glanced at her phone to find no response.

—I thought old men got up early and went to bed early, isn't that the deal?—

She grinned as she sent it off, anticipating his sarcastic response. She finished her bagel in her room and reviewed the file. Nothing was new to her, but Remi saved it just in case. Around eight, she checked her phone again, and still no response from Desmond.

—*Hey, everything okay? Didn't think you liked to sleep in.*—

As fifteen minutes ticked by, Remi started pacing, chewing on her thumb.

—*Graves, if you're playing a joke, I'm missing the punchline.*—

Nothing. She called, but there was no answer. She sent another text.

—*Check in.*—

Another five minutes and she got dressed, threw on her jacket, and jogged down to the garage. The tracker still showed him in his house, but not moving. On the way, she texted one last time.

—*Check in or it's guns blazing. Not a joke.*—

She got to the garage, shoving the door aside. She almost hit Alec, who jumped back, his eyes wide. "Everything okay?"

"I don't know." She threw her leg over the seat of her bike and called once again. Still no answer. "Damn!" she snarled into her helmet before peeling out onto the street.

Remi broke thirteen traffic laws on the drive to Desmond's building, including splitting the lanes and speeding—so much speeding. She made it to his place in record time, parking on the sidewalk. Ignoring Peter, she bypassed the elevator and ran up the seven flights of stairs to his floor.

The door was locked when she tried it. Remi drew

her gun, listening for anything inside the apartment. When she heard nothing unusual, she knocked. "Graves?"

No response.

She used the key he'd reluctantly given her the second day, ghosting in and locking the door behind her. Keeping her gun ready, she stepped forward, looking for any sign of something being off.

When she got to the edge of Desmond's kitchen, a figure moved in the unlit space. Remi reacted, lifting her gun, finger hovering over the trigger before she saw the profile and realized who it was.

Desmond never moved, not even when Remi swore. She uncocked the gun and slid it back into her holster. "Desmond, what the hell?!" She slammed her hand into the switch.

The lights threw him into relief as he leaned against the counter. He still wore the same suit from the funeral, more wrinkled than yesterday. The crystal glass in his hand was too full of amber liquid to be a casual drink. She checked the rest of the house, pissed that he was okay, and relieved for the same reason. In a few moments, she determined they were alone. Desmond seemed fine physically, which made the relief fade. Her hands fisted at her sides as she glared at him.

"Why the hell didn't you answer your phone?! We had a deal!" When she didn't get an answer, she stepped forward. Beneath her boot, glass crunched. She looked down to see a shattered glass that would have matched the one in his hand.

Remi took a moment, peering closer at him. He was half drunk, but the lines on his face were different from anger. This was fear.

Immediately, everything inside shifted, the anger directed within, but now wasn't the time. She took a deep breath and looked up at him. "What happened?"

He didn't move; he didn't even seem to know she was there.

"Desmond." She placed her hand on his arm, keeping her voice soft.

He looked up, first to where her hand rested on his arm, then up to her face. His eyes were red and hazy, and he didn't say anything. He gestured with his glass to the table, where a manila envelope sat. The top was open, and a photograph sat facedown over it.

Remi picked it up, seeing Ashley's face in the photo. She was smiling down at her phone, unaware that someone was following her. Over her face, scrawled in familiar silver ink, Remi read:

Do you care so little for your family? You'd choose your career over her?

Letting out a sigh, she put the photo back down where it was.

"Where'd you get this?" she asked, fighting hard to keep her voice calm.

"From my bag." He sounded hoarse, either from disuse, or too much use, and she prayed for the former. "Yesterday."

Yesterday. Fourteen hours of him dealing with this alone. Her gut twisted again. "Why didn't you call?"

He shrugged, one shoulder lifting an inch. "What could you have done?"

"My job, Graves," she said, taking the photo and putting it back in the envelope, out of sight. "Make sure you aren't alone. Look out for you. Keep you from drinking the good stuff over bad shit."

He scoffed, downing the glass in his hands and reaching for the bottle. Remi grabbed it and kept it out of his reach. "You've had enough."

Desmond stared at her, then put the glass down a little harder than he should have. He held her gaze for a long moment, and she wasn't sure if he was going to argue or try to grab the bottle or yell—

Instead, he took in a deep breath, hanging his head as he braced himself against the counter. Then he looked up. "They're going after Ashley."

Lies didn't do anything but make him less prepared. "But we might know why. Landon is on your docket this week. Hitman for the Blackheart gang, which is currently run by—"

"Delaney," he finished.

"Exactly."

He was quiet, and Remi let the silence linger. He ran his hand over his face. "What am I supposed to do?" he asked, his voice rough but for different reasons.

"You never listen to anything I say. Why's now any different?"

"Because I don't know."

Remi chewed her lip, then leaned against the counter next to him. "You do know, hotshot." She bumped her shoulder against him. "What're your options?"

Desmond didn't hesitate, knowing the same things she did. "Drop the case and let him get away with it."

"What'll happen?" She stared at his profile. The sun was high, cutting through the curtained windows. It started to drive away the heaviness of the picture.

"More people will die," he said after a moment. "There's no guarantee they'll leave me and Ashley alone. No guarantee they won't do this again."

"And if you don't stop?"

"He'll be convicted. But I run the risk of someone coming after Ashley."

"And you."

He didn't say anything. Remi stared at him, knowing he was about to hate her a little bit. "There's only one option you can live with. And you know it."

He glared at her, the first moment of real emotion from him since she'd walked in. "Ashley is more important than any stranger."

"I'll have protection put on her. She'll be safe."

"I'm not choosing someone else over her. But if I can bring Delaney down, there won't be a threat to her. And taking out his cleaner is a blow to any gang," he said, trying to convince himself as much as he was her.

"I agree."

"Archer, I'm not—this isn't about me—" he started, his voice tight.

She put her hand on his shoulder. "You love your sister. I know. You'll do anything to protect her, but sometimes that's a choice between a rock and a bullet. It's a hard choice. I know you're doing this for her. For everyone in this city."

She allowed him another moment of silence, letting him come to terms with his decision. Then, she squeezed his arm and let go. "Why don't you take a shower and get cleaned up. You smell like a dive bar. I'm gonna call in some backup, get someone on Ashley's place, and we can figure out what to do after that, okay?"

"What kind of dive bar serves fifteen-year-old scotch?" he inquired, some light returning to his eyes.

"Fifteen years, huh?" she repeated, eyeing the bottle in her hand. She took a long swig, which almost made him smile, then grabbed the cap and spun it on. "Go on. I've got this."

"I know." His hand grazed over her shoulder before he walked to his bedroom and shut the door.

As soon as he was gone, Remi pulled out her phone and dialed.

"Exceptional Security, this is—"

"Get Thomas right now."

****

Remi paced in Desmond's kitchen, as Thomas stared down at the letter on the counter. "We'll put security on his sister," he said, looking up at her, who had yet to stop moving. "But I don't know why—"

"How did it get here?" she hissed, glancing over her shoulder to make sure the bathroom door was still shut. The water was going and had been since Thomas arrived. "I check his mail. I check his place. We didn't go to the office, but I check that, too. There was nothing in the car."

"What other option is there?" he asked, eyeing her.

"Someone slipped it in his mail after I checked? Or…" She trailed off as realization hit. "Or someone got close enough to get it in his bag. I would've been right there and not seen it. Dammit." She covered her mouth. "They got close enough to touch him, and I didn't see it."

"We knew the funeral was risky," Thomas reminded her. "And our biggest suspect was there. Could he have gotten close enough to—"

"No." She was certain about that, at least. "No, Delaney never got close enough."

"All right. We'll run recognition on the rest of the funeral party, and I'll have Samara tail the sister. We'll fill her in on everything that's going on. Mr. Singh set up security downstairs that will do real-time facial recognition. If we narrow down the targets, we can keep anyone we don't want in from entering." He cleared his throat, fidgeted with the paper for a moment, then looked at her. "Are you certain you're okay here?"

Remi, who still hadn't stopped pacing, glanced up. "What the hell is that supposed to mean?"

"I mean that…you seem a little *attached* to Mr. Graves. I'm wondering if you're able to remain clear-headed enough to do the job." His voice strengthened as he spoke, though she stopped and glared at him.

"Back up. Are you accusing me of being too invested in keeping a decent guy alive?"

"You know that's not what I'm saying. But I worry that you may be getting a little too close and—"

"I'm in control. I can do the job."

He nodded after a moment, dropping the subject. "I'll take this letter back, see if we can pick up anything from it. It's the most recent, so there may be some trace evidence we can pick up on. I'll keep you updated on everything else."

"Thanks," she said, sharper than normal.

Thomas took the letter and headed to the door, stopping to turn before he opened it. "If you need anything, we're here."

"Thank you." That one was a little more sincere.

With a quick nod, he left. Remi locked the door and rested her forehead against the wood, taking a couple of deep breaths.

She'd been in this business a while now, and she'd dealt with dangerous situations before. She'd been in war zones and at the wrong end of a gun. She'd almost died several times, dragging herself back from the brink. But this morning had been terrifying. The not knowing. She clenched her fist, getting rid of the last vestiges of fear, the last faint tremors. She had to be calm. Desmond needed her to be calm.

She walked into the living room and sat at his piano, running her fingers across the cover. The mirror-like surface of the wood caught her fingerprints, so she wiped them off. Carefully, she lifted the cover without leaving more marks. Grazing her hands over the keys, she found a familiar position. With only a few mistakes, she managed to bring forth a few bars of a familiar song into the empty room. The mindless action soothed her, and her breath moved in time with the music, slow and steady.

She heard the bathroom door open but didn't stop until she'd reached the end of the first verse. The last chord echoed a little, drifting in the sunlight.

"I didn't know you played."

His voice sounded calmer now, and she smiled. "I don't anymore," she said, turning to face him. "But sometimes—"

She broke off, almost swallowing her tongue as she looked at him. Gone were the suits and dress coats. In their place, Desmond wore tight jeans and a sweater that looked so soft, she wanted to run her hands all over him. *It.*

Remi cleared her throat and looked back down at the piano. "Sometimes it's nice." She covered the keys again and stood. Looking at him, more prepared this time, she noted the bags under his eyes. But the lines weren't as entrenched on his skin, and his eyes were brighter and sharper now.

"Thomas has come and gone. He's gonna get security on Ashley, so she'll be safe. He's taking the letter back to see whatever we can get off of it. You and I are making sure we put Landon away for a good long time. Can you handle that?"

He nodded, turning to his desk and pulling out the file. Stacking other papers out of the way, he retrieved other folders from his briefcase. As he made room for her, he said, "It would be a pleasure."

"I knew you had a vindictive streak." She sat at the chair he'd pulled over for her.

With a low chuckle, he nodded. "Well, it helps that you've made things easier. Without you, I imagine I'd be…a lot less capable right now. You always know what to do."

If he'd seen her panicking, he would've thought something very different. This was better. He needed her to be a rock, so that's exactly what she'd do.

"I've got your back." She grabbed the folder and opened it. "Let's put him away."

****

"What I don't get is, why now?"

Desmond leaned back in his chair, linking his hands behind his head. His gaze followed Remi as she paced around his room. Discarded boxes from their lunch occupied his kitchen counter, with spots of orange chicken sauce dotting the dark marble. He recalled their conversation earlier.

"What do you mean you don't like orange chicken?" he'd asked.

"It's not personal." She laughed, leaning away as he held the box out to her.

"What kind of person hates orange chicken?"

"This kind."

She'd hung her jacket over the back of his couch, the tank top clinging to every curve on her torso. Desmond forced his eyes upward, to where she flipped a blade over her fingers, still waiting for an answer.

"Because he got caught," he said.

"Yeah, but so did Delaney's bookkeeper, three months ago."

"I know. I was on the case."

"I know." She glared at him as she continued to pace. "But that led to the cops taking down some thirty-five percent of Delaney's businesses. That crippled him. So why didn't he try to threaten you then? Why all this over a subpar hitman who was stupid enough to get himself caught?"

"Convenience. Delaney was looking for a reason to come after me. Last wishes of dear old dad," Desmond suggested. "Any number of reasons."

Remi shrugged, clearly unconvinced, but didn't push it. Desmond kept his eyes on her for a long moment, but she remained quiet. He turned back to drafting his arguments for court tomorrow. "What surprises me is that Delaney is choosing to threaten over such a simple case. Landon confessed. This case is open and shut. Anyone could close it."

"Why'd he confess?"

"No choice." He turned to the next page, tapping the back of his pen against his desk. "He was found leaving the scene of the crime, with the murder weapon, and his prints on the body matched the ones in the system." He shuffled through a few pages, then handed her a photograph of the crime scene. It wasn't even included in most of his arguments since the case was so clear. "Look for yourself."

She came over and grabbed it, bringing it back to the window with a frown.

He covered a lot in the next few minutes, slipping into the prosecutor's mindset. He'd drafted the few questions he'd have for Landon before Remi walked over, the photo almost at her nose. "You have a coroner's report?"

"Come again?" he asked, not quite paying attention.

"Coroner's report. Do you have it?"

With a sigh, he grabbed the report and handed it to her. She began reading it, even as he summed it up for her. "Two in the head. Matched the gun found on Landon. Classic execution style—"

He fell silent as she dropped the papers in front of him. "He's lying."

"What?"

"Landon's *lying*. He may have killed the guy, but he wasn't alone. Someone else was there." She leaned over his shoulder, putting the photo on top of his papers. "Look. This entrance wound is a mirror image of this one. Unless he shot him with two hands." She bent her wrists at an odd angle. "Or he got on the ground. And where did he get rid of the second gun? There's no way it makes sense. Unless—"

"Unless there was someone else there. Someone Landon felt he had to protect," Desmond finished, picking up the photo. How the hell did he miss this?

"And if he's willing to go down protecting

someone, it must someone Delaney doesn't want you investigating at all. They must be someone important to his organization. Even more important than his bookie or his cleaner. Someone worth threatening the hotshot lawyer on the case."

He smiled, cutting his eyes up at her. "You think I'm hot?"

"That's not what I said." A faint smile began to appear on her face, dispelling some of the tension.

"It's what you meant."

"Is this you in a good mood?" she asked. "Because you are super annoying in a good mood, and I hate it. Go back to being whiny and dramatic."

"That's not a no." He leaned a little nearer to her, letting his smile fade into a smirk as he enjoyed the flush on her cheeks.

Remi rolled her eyes. "So we need to figure out who Landon is protecting and why they matter so much to Delaney. I'll put Gemma on it—"

"I've got it."

She leaned back, meeting his eyes from a safer distance. "You've got it, huh?"

"He faces off against me in court tomorrow. I'll find out. Your thing is guns blazing. Mine is getting people to admit what they didn't want to."

"You think you can get him to admit who else was there?" Remi asked, her brow arched.

"Just like I got you to admit you think I'm hot."

She smiled. "Screw you."

****

It was late when Remi grabbed her jacket and pulled it on to leave. She'd helped Desmond run through potential questions. By the time they were finished, she had to admit, he knew what he was doing.

His eyes darted around the room several times as she started making moves to the door. Desmond was quiet as he walked her out. The dark hallway made it hard to see the lines deepening on his face, but not impossible.

Remi stopped at the door. "If you want, I can stay here tonight."

Desmond smiled, the lines still there, but more manageable. "If I have to be in court tomorrow, I need some sleep. You being here won't help in that regard."

"Bold, Graves."

He shrugged. "Facts are facts."

She laughed then, leaning up and kissing his cheek. For a moment, the briefest breath, she hesitated, there against his skin. But Thomas's comment came rushing back, and she thought maybe…maybe he had a point.

"You need anything—"

A tired smile appeared on his face at the repetition. "Guns blazing."

"I mean it. Anything."

"I know." His hand lifted like he was going to touch her face. He dropped it down, taking a small step back. "Goodnight."

"'Night, Des. See you tomorrow."

She walked down the stairwell, hands in her pockets and head bowed as she mulled over the day. A long day.

Still, when she got outside, she didn't get onto her bike immediately. She crossed the street and stood in an alley. It was far enough back that she could see the glow from the living room windows on the seventh floor. She watched, chewing on her nail until the lights went out. Checking the phone, she saw that Desmond was in his bedroom. Throwing up a quick request to whoever might listen, she hoped he got some rest.

Soon after, she got on her bike and headed home. But her thoughts remained at the seventh-story penthouse.

Chapter Six

Remi had long ago gotten over herself and admitted Desmond Graves was an impressive man. She'd seen him at his worst, and for the most part he remained dignified, controlled, and sure of himself. A large part of her respected him for how high he'd risen despite the anchors of his past. The word *admirable* suited him.

Then Remi met the courtroom version of Desmond and—

Holy. *Shit*.

Bad ass in a suit worked. Real well.

He marched—didn't walk—through the double doors of the courtroom, with her not on his heels. From the moment he opened his mouth, it was clear he owned the room. Every eye was on him. Everyone in attendance, jurors and audience, hung onto his every word. He was the sarcastic, quick-talking, didn't-take-shit kind of lawyer she could respect.

"Am I to understand there is no plea deal?" the judge asked.

"Correct, Your Honor," Desmond answered, his eyes on the papers in front of him. "Plea deals are for those who feel guilt."

Remi smothered her smile from her spot behind him. The courtroom wasn't crowded, so she had been able to sit in the front row. The defense looked tired already, and it had only begun. Relaxing into the bench, she got ready for one hell of a ride.

"Your name is Samuel Landon?" Desmond asked, hand in one pocket as he stood in front of the man in the witness stand.

"Yes."

Landon looked older than his stated age, with a drawn face and dark, lank hair hanging on both sides of his face. The orange jumpsuit didn't do much for him, but she doubted a tailored suit would've helped. Plus, his greasy skin and ferret eyes didn't do the man any favors.

"Thirty-four years old?"

"Yes."

"Right-handed?"

"Uh, yes?"

"You have to think about that?" Desmond said, shooting the questions at him.

"No." Landon frowned at him. "But I don't see the point."

"Luckily, it's not up to you to determine relevance." Desmond continued his questions. "You're a hitman?"

"I've killed for money."

"And how long have you been killing for James Delaney's money?"

"Objection!" cried the defense. "That's a leading question."

"Leading to the truth."

"Mr. Graves..." The judge warned, with a smile, apparently used to this type of behavior from Desmond.

While Remi bit her lip to hide her grin, Desmond smirked, the condescending glance shot to the defense not apologetic at all. "Withdrawn."

Didn't matter that he'd withdrawn, Remi felt the jury was already leaning toward the prosecution. He looked back to Landon. "You single?"

"Excuse me?"

"I asked, are you single?"

"I'm sure as hell not interested in you," Landon spat.

"Mr. Landon." The judge's tone was sharper than when she'd addressed Desmond. "Answer the question."

Landon rolled his eyes. "Yes, I'm single."

"So Vanessa Masoft, who visited you several times in prison, isn't your girlfriend?"

Though Landon remained quiet, he continued to glare at Desmond.

"You're either lying to me or lying to her." Desmond glanced at the jury. "Don't know which is worse." That elicited a brief laugh from a few of the jurors.

"She's a girl I was seeing. I don't do girlfriends," Landon finally said.

As Masoft wasn't on the list they'd compiled last night, Remi immediately emailed Gemma, requesting a search on the woman. Gemma almost immediately sent back information on Masoft's rap sheet: petty crimes, shoplifting. Nothing serious.

"Charming," Desmond retorted. "What does Vanessa Masoft do?"

"Me."

The judge snapped. "Mr. Landon, have some decency, or I'll hold you in contempt."

Landon shifted in the wooden chair, his eyes

darting around. "She's in retail. Clothing."

"Nice girl?"

"Nice enough."

Desmond hummed. "Right. How much can you bench, Landon?"

"Are you looking for a date or something?"

"Mr. Landon!"

"Thanks, but no thanks," Desmond said, speaking over the judge's ire. "I'm unavailable as of right now. Just curiosity."

Remi tried not to flush at that comment, keeping her eyes on Desmond as he stared at Landon.

"I can bench two hundred pounds."

"And you're right-handed?" Desmond asked again.

"Yes."

"And your preferred gun of choice is…?"

Landon's mouth opened, then shut again, and Remi grinned. Desmond was getting close.

"I don't have one," he finally said.

"Sure you don't," Desmond said, winking at Landon. Then, his tone changed. "Are you aware that James Delaney's bookie was convicted of tax evasion a few months ago?"

Landon glared and didn't answer.

"Mr. Landon," the judge said.

"That's fine, Your Honor. He doesn't have to answer." Desmond stepped up to the witness box and leaned on the banister, speaking as if it were only him and Landon in the room. "As a result of said conviction, we obtained access to all sorts of classified information. The reason I asked if you were on Delaney's payroll, is because we found several payments made to your name."

"So? That doesn't—"

"And then corroborated those payments with your bank account."

Landon fell silent.

"So, I'll ask again, with context, and without leading the witness. How long have you been receiving money from James Delaney for undisclosed services?"

"Seven years," Landon muttered.

"Great. So glad we're all on the same page." Desmond went back to his desk and grabbed a piece of paper. "Now, looking at the payments, I'm seeing some regular occurrences of payments of $15,000. Not bad for a hired gun."

"Objection," the defense attorney said.

Desmond nodded, waving his hands as he discarded that line of questioning. "Withdrawn. Every payment aligns with the death of some opponent of Delaney. Rival gang lords, politicians, lawyers…" He looked at the jury and shrugged. "I'm sure that's a coincidence."

"Objection!" the defense repeated. "Is there a question here?"

"Several in fact, but I'm giving some background information." Desmond glanced at the defense. "You received consistent payments over the last seven years. But in the last three months, those payments have diminished. You're paid the same number of times, but you're making less. The fact that you're here tells me you haven't quite retired from whatever work you do, wet or dry."

"Objection!"

"Are you still working for Delaney?" Desmond asked.

"Yes." Landon frowned at his attorney, clearly agitated by the line of questioning.

"Then why aren't you getting paid the full amount?"

"What the hell does this have to do with anything?" Landon shouted. "You concerned about my tax bracket?"

"Oh, not in the slightest," Desmond said. "I just notice that several payments have begun going to another person—half the amount, at the same time as your jobs. Who's receiving the other half?"

Landon got to his feet, ignoring the cops as they stepped forward toward him. Remi tensed, her hand going to her waist, but remained in her chair. Landon shouted, "Look, I'm on trial for killing McCulloch, and I've admitted to that, so what the hell are you trying to do?! I'm guilty, so send me the hell away from you!"

"Because you're lying, Mr. Landon!" Desmond shouted, startling Landon into silence and stillness.

The jury stared at him, open-mouthed and rapt. Even the defense attorney stared at Desmond, confusion raging in his eyes. Remi leaned forward as Desmond leveled a glare at Landon, his words audible to everyone in the room.

"You're a liar, Mr. Landon." Desmond's voice was terrifyingly calm. "You shot Evan McCulloch, true. But you've been training someone else to do your work. Someone new and inexperienced, who was also there. They also shot McCulloch. They are the reason you were caught. And I'm going to find out who."

The banging of the judge's gavel did little to stem the insanity. The defense was on his feet, shouting for a recess and among the chaos, Desmond turned around and smirked at Remi.

Her stomach did the tiniest of flips as she smiled back at him.

She was in *sooooo* much trouble.

****

Remi put her chopsticks down on her plate, shaking her head at him.

"What?" Desmond's fork hovered above the plate.

"Are you always like that in the courtroom?" she asked.

It was about an hour after the judge declared a recess. The defense lawyer, Michael Spenser, a low-level grunt on Delaney's payroll, pitched a fit over Desmond's attack on his client. In response, the judge granted a recess until after the lunch break to recover. Knowing Landon was on the ropes, Desmond felt confident enough to go out for lunch. He and Remi had stumbled upon a small sushi bar, busy enough that they had to wait a few minutes. After they squeezed into a small booth in the back, three rolls and a pot of green tea showed up in record time.

He didn't ask what she meant.

In the courtroom, where Des knew all the rules better than his opponents, he felt confident. Untouchable. It was the only place he'd beaten his father. It was the only place he could take down the nightmares of his past, metaphorical or physical. He was invincible in the courtroom, and he knew it. So he acted like it. And it had an effect—the jury loved him, the judge let him get away with more, defense hated him—it was all in his favor.

He owned that room. And that mood tended to follow him wherever he went.

"Yes," he said. "Impressed?"

Her brow vaulted up, the corner of her mouth following suit. "A little."

"I'll have to try harder."

He grabbed another piece of sushi with his fork and Remi huffed. "I can't believe you refuse to use chopsticks."

"Forks are an amazing invention."

Her mouth twitched up in a smile. "I don't want to get into this again."

"Then admit I'm right."

"Never."

Remi paid after they finished up and walked back to the courthouse. They got through security fine, as Remi flashed the papers that allowed her to carry her firearms. Desmond was familiar with the process. A few years ago, he and Ashley had police security and the officers carried similar paperwork.

Remi paused inside the main doors after security, glancing at her phone. "I'll be right back."

While she stepped around the corner to take the call, Desmond took the time to rummage through his bag to get his papers back in order.

"Well, isn't it the man of the hour?"

Half-recognizing the voice, Desmond looked up, an automatic and polite response was on his lips. "Thanks, but—"

James Delaney stood in front of him, his face anything but kind.

"No, thanks," Desmond finished.

Delaney took a step closer, leaning toward him. "What do you think you're doing, Desi?"

His instinct was to take a step back. Conjuring up

the image of Remi facing off with Delaney at the funeral, Desmond stayed in place and lifted his chin. "My job."

"Have you forgotten exactly what I'm capable of?"

"No. Want to go in there and discuss it?" Desmond gestured to the courtroom. "I'm sure there will be several interested parties."

Delaney's lip quivered. "If you think you can threaten me, I'll—"

"No." Desmond interrupted. "You won't do anything. Because I'm the only one keeping you from behind bars. If I speak, with my past, my reputation, they'd listen."

"You won't admit to your shame."

"How confident are you about that?" Desmond asked, taking a step closer. "I don't see your goons standing by. Still feeling brave alone?"

"I can destroy you, boy. You're alone here and—"

"I'm not a boy any longer."

"And not alone."

Delaney flinched, twisting to look back as Remi appeared from behind him. Her hand was on his shoulder, her knuckles white as she ground her fingers into Delaney's suitcoat. He tried to lean away from her, but she held him fast.

"You owe the man an apology." Though her voice was calm, Desmond knew enough of Remi to recognize the dangerous, flat tone. Delaney wasn't.

"If you think that—"

Desmond saw the muscles in her arm flex, then Delaney broke off the protest with a satisfying squeal of pain. Remi spoke over him. "That didn't sound like an apology."

Pale and panting, Delaney still glared at her. "Bitch, I will take everything you love—"

Smiling, Remi leaned forward to hiss in his ear. "And I'll take your arm. Apologize."

Delaney turned back to Desmond, hatred burning in his eyes. "I *apologize*, Desi."

Desmond didn't respond, but Remi released Delaney's arm. He shook it out, his hand dangling, then he opened his mouth—

"Just give me a reason." Remi's hand was on her hip, and she took a half step to get between him and Desmond.

Delaney stared at them, his face glimmering with sweat from either pain or anger, it was unclear. "You two deserve each other," he spat, before turning on his heel and shoving past someone to the doors.

Remi waited until he was gone, then faced Desmond, her brow already drawing together. "Are you—"

"I'm fine."

"I'm sorry, that was Thomas and—"

"Remi, I'm fine."

She stared at him for a moment, then nodded, her breath huffing out of her. "Thomas said Vanessa Masoft hasn't been at work the past few days, but her attendance was pretty spotty before that. Delaney might have her on the payroll for this, she could be the one Landon's training." She shrugged, her frown deepening.

"But?"

"Something smells wrong about all this. The timing, the people...I don't know. Something's messed up." She rubbed her forehead, that frown still present.

"Come on." He walked them away from the courtroom and down a narrow hallway, into an unused room. The small desk and phoneline inside were helpful for lawyers who needed to prep or confer with their clients. Leaving the door cracked open, he faced her. "What's wrong with the timing?"

"Des, you have court—" she argued, waving over her shoulder.

"Don't worry about me. Talk it through. What's wrong with the timing?"

She stared at him for a moment, before taking a deep breath. "It's just too strange. Doesn't line up with Delaney's rise to the head of the gang. Doesn't line up with your father's discovery of you throwing the case. The beginning of the notes doesn't line up with anything at all. Nothing."

"Landon's case—"

"No, I went back, and it doesn't." Remi paced in the small space as best she could. "The first note, the very first one, was sent three months ago—two days *before* they arrested Landon." She ran her hands through her hair. "And Vanessa? Petty theft and small-time crimes, then she graduates to a hired gun? I don't think so. And why would Delaney be going through so much trouble to protect her? She's a nobody. No connections. No money. No family. Why bother?"

Desmond nodded, admitting the truth of all those things. "Then what is it?"

"I don't know." She ran her fingers through her hair and turned to face him. The anger was there, but not meant for him. "I don't know, and that's what worries me."

Taking a moment, Desmond inhaled through his

nose. "All right. We know Delaney's involved. Let's see what we can get from Landon, at least."

Remi still looked concerned, so Desmond put his hand on her shoulder as he led her out of the room. The brightness of the hallway made him blink. "Archer, you keep me from the guns, and I'll get you the information."

She chuckled. "Not exactly how the protection thing is supposed to go."

"I'm a modern man."

"That's for damn sure," she muttered.

"Desi?"

Desmond stopped and turned, seeing his sister walking toward them. "Ash, what are you doing here?"

"Rode with a friend who had a parole check," she said. "You in court today?"

"Yeah. Landon's case." He frowned. "Which friend?"

"Not a big deal." She looked between the two of them, and Desmond realized he still had his hand on Remi's shoulder.

He dropped it, stepping a little closer to Ashley. "If you need help or something—"

She laughed, tossing her hair back a little. "I can take care of myself, Desi. Don't worry about me."

"I always do."

She smiled, then leaned up to kiss his cheek, turning away. "I'll give you a call later, once I'm done moving my stuff. You can tell me about the case."

"Sure. Bye, Ash."

Remi was watching Ashley go when Desmond turned back to her. She blinked and refocused on Desmond when he sighed. "Doing all right?"

"Peachy."

She smiled at him, and Desmond felt the remnants of the tension from the encounter with Delaney disappear. "You got this, hotshot. I'll watch your back."

He smiled. "I know."

She opened the courtroom door and waved him in.

Desmond straightened his tie and stepped inside.

****

Landon wiped his face. The matted tissue he held left little white bits on his forehead. Remi chewed her nail, watching Desmond pace in front of him.

They had admitted the pictures of the shooting and an expert corroborated what Remi had said. Landon's financials were part of the evidence already, and now Desmond was wringing Landon out to dry.

"What's the kickback on a Smith and Wesson .357?"

Landon scoffed. "Like a fucking horse."

"So you've fired such a weapon?"

Landon flinched, his eyes darting to his attorney. "I, uh—"

"The answer you're looking for is yes," Desmond stage whispered.

"Objection, there's no evi—"

"There's a plethora of evidence," Desmond interrupted Spenser's continued objections. "As the ballistics expert previously testified, that was the gun fired at the scene of the crime. And your witness had confessed to shooting the victim."

"Overruled," the judge added, nodding at Desmond to continue.

"So, that's the weapon you fired?" Desmond asked, slipping into that quick-talk action again. Remi leaned forward, her eyes following the exchange.

"Yes."

"And you used your right hand?"

"Yes."

"So you shot him in the left side of his head?"

"Uh…yes?"

"What about the wound, on the right side?"

"I did that after."

"So you hauled him back up, shot him a second time, then let him drop?"

"Yes."

"We found no evidence of the body being moved."

"I'm real good."

"You were caught," Desmond reminded him.

"So, I shot him after he fell."

"And you shot him in the right side of the head?" Desmond repeated.

"Yes. Wait, no. I mean—"

"Did you shoot him right-handed in the left, or left-handed in the right?"

"I don't—I just shoot people, okay?"

"Like a hitman?"

Landon dropped the tissue and grasped the banister. "Yes! No!"

"Two wounds. One hitman." Desmond held his hands out like he was weighing the two pieces of evidence.

Landon stared at his hands, his eyes lighting up. "Both hands."

"Pardon?"

"I shot him with both hands. Two guns. Two hands." Landon sat back on the chair, chest heaving.

Desmond nodded, a faint smirk on his face. "Two

guns, huh?" He slipped both hands into his pockets and looked away from Landon as he walked in front of the witness stand. "So where's the other gun?"

"What?"

"We only found one gun at the scene. So your partner shot after you?"

"No—"

"So they shot them before?" Desmond spun on his heel to face him. Remi was on the edge of her seat.

"Yes—wait, no!"

"Which is it?"

"I shot him!"

"And your partner shot him the second time?"

"No, she—" Landon broke off with a gasp. Remi grinned.

"Ah." Desmond stopped and held up his finger. "So your partner was there. And she's a woman. Good to know. No further questions at the moment."

Landon paled; the defense attorney rose; the jury murmured. The judge banged her gavel. "Order! Defense, approach the bench, please."

Desmond took his seat at the prosecution's table directly in front of Remi, looking completely unruffled. He threw one arm along the bar behind him and glanced back at her. "Told you I could break him," he murmured, confidence oozing off of every syllable.

She couldn't help her smile. "No name yet, hotshot."

The judge and Spenser exchanged a few words before the judge motioned for Desmond to join them. He stood, winking at Remi as he did so. Crossing to the stand, he grinned at Landon.

The jury had shuffled out, but the audience

continued talking amongst themselves. Through it all, Remi heard the doors open and glanced behind instinctively. A disheveled blonde woman entered the courtroom, raised her hand to point—

No, to aim.

Remi couldn't get in a full breath—not before she moved, launching into the aisle and drawing her weapon. Vanessa Masoft, Remi recognized her from the picture, got off one shot before Remi shot twice.

No choice. No other option. No hesitation. She didn't miss.

Vanessa dropped, two in the head, eyes still open.

From behind her, screaming began and only got louder. The attack was so sudden that half the crowd was only beginning to realize what happened. Remi couldn't hear anything over the roar of her pulse pounding in her head.

Remi stared at Vanessa, her eyes wide because she knew—

She'd heard Vanessa's bullet hitting someone.

She'd heard the grunt of pain, the sound of a body falling. She stared at the body and tried to get the nerve to turn around.

Her chest hurt; she couldn't breathe.

Who was it…Was it…?

Turn around.

Turn around!

Chapter Seven

Desmond never registered the sound of the courtroom door opening.

He did notice when Remi got out of her seat and lunged toward the center of the room.

He noticed as a woman approached, her gun raised.

He noticed Remi getting between the gun and him.

He noticed the lack of hesitation on Remi's part as she moved to protect him. He noticed that she was only wearing her usual clothes. But no bulletproof vest, no body armor.

Fear overwhelmed him when he saw the gun aimed at him. But it was nothing compared to what he felt when he realized how unprotected Remi was.

He noticed the sounds of three bullets, the echoes of which shot through him, shaking him to his bones. His vision tilted as he took a step forward, toward the shooter, toward the gun—

Toward Remi.

The surrounding screams brought his focus back. His vision clarified, and he heard the sound of someone slumping to the ground.

It wasn't Remi.

Shoulders rigid, she didn't move, simply stared at the body on the floor. Desmond took another step toward her. "Remi?" he called, unsure if she would even hear him over the clamor.

As she turned, she didn't hide the fear on her face. Her eyes darted over him, looking for an injury as he did the same to her. As soon as she realized he was okay, she looked past him, and Desmond did the same.

Landon was out of his chair.

Desmond followed Remi back to the witness stand. Cops were starting to charge into the room, shouting orders. She paid them no mind.

Sam Landon was dead. One, right in the forehead, eyes still wide and stuck in the same expression of shock. Desmond found his breath was coming a little shorter as he stared down at the body.

Remi looked up to where the judge should have been, then leaned behind the dais and found the jurist crouched behind the podium. "It's fine. You're safe."

Remi turned toward the shooter's body, riffling through her pockets. She found nothing, no wallet, no ID. Then, cursing under her breath, she grabbed Desmond by the arm. "We're getting you out of here."

Guards stationed at the door tried to stop her, but she threw an Exceptional Security business card at them and told them to call her office for any questions. They pushed past the crowds and paparazzi assigned to cover the Landon trial. As rumors sprouted, panic ensued; everyone rushed to evacuate the building.

Remi kept her hand on Desmond's arm, pulling and shielding him at the same time. He felt cold, close to freezing. But he was wearing a suit. Why was he so cold?

They made it to the parking lot on the east side of the courthouse just as the ambulances arrived, sirens blaring. Police had already moved to block off the area.

Remi got him into the car before walking around to

the driver's seat. She slammed the door shut and screeched out from the parking spot without a word. Once they hit the highway, she used the hands-free option on the dash to place a call.

"Get Thomas…"

"Yeah, Remi, what's up?" a male voice answered after several clicks at the other end.

"Shut up and listen."

"All right."

"Masoft just walked into court with a gun. I took care of her. She didn't give me a choice." Her voice remained flat, detached. "Landon's dead. I've got Des with me. We're coming to you. It's going to be a disaster. I left them a card, but I had to get him out of there…Send anyone you can spare to help clean this up. And figure out how the hell Masoft got past security with a gun…We'll be there soon."

She hit the icon on the dash to end the call then shouted, "Shit!"

The totality of the situation hit Desmond with a sledgehammer. He closed his eyes and leaned back against the headrest. They drove in silence, weaving through traffic until they parked outside Exceptional Security. Remi motioned for him to stay in his seat. He did as she told him, his breathing sounding harsh in the quiet. She went around to the passenger side, her eyes continuing to scan in a three-sixty motion of her head as she opened the door for him. Pushing him into a crouch, she half-pushed, half-urged him forward. Once they were safely in the lobby, she let out a huff of air, her shoulders softening.

Gemma wasn't at the desk, but Remi reached behind and grabbed a card. She didn't hand it to

Desmond but led him back to the doors they went through the last time, up the same stairs, and down the hall to a door near the end. She was already on her phone, clearly trying to figure out what happened. Opening the door, she ushered him on, and stayed right on his heels.

Still cold, he shivered as the door clicked shut behind them, echoing like thunder. An echo of what had happened. And he was back in the courtroom, staring at Remi in front of the gun.

Then he was back on the sidewalk in front of his house, bullets cracking through the air. He heard them hitting him, hitting her—

His lungs closed, he couldn't breathe, no air, no nothing. He grabbed the desk in the corner; he couldn't see from the darkness claiming him. He didn't see Remi move, couldn't hear her, but he felt her presence.

"Hey, Jesus, hey, Des?" She grabbed his arms and held them above his head. "Deep breaths, okay? You're having a panic attack. I need you to breathe. Deep breaths in and out. Focus on my voice."

The darkness began to fade, and he could see her in front of him. She modeled the breathing as she talked him through it, her blue eyes focused on him. "Tell me something you can hear."

His teeth were still chattering, and it was freezing. The humming was all around him. "A.C."

"Good. What's something you can smell?"

Her jacket swung and creaked as she held his arms up, still, not moving. His lungs were starting to feel a little more open. "Leather."

"Something you can see."

"You."

"Details, smartass. I'm trying to ground you, here."

"Blonde hair. Blue eyes. Black leather. A scar above your right eye."

His lungs opened a bit; he breathed easier; his teeth stopped chattering. Remi let go of his arms, but caught his hands, holding onto him as she searched his eyes. "You good?"

He felt weak. Wrung out. "Fine."

She squeezed his hands. "Des."

The faint reprimand was there, and he sighed. "I'll be fine. That was just…"

"Terrifying?"

Hearing it from her, the experienced mercenary, the trained security, helped. His feelings weren't pathetic or weak, he wasn't wrong. He was normal, and this was a normal reaction to someone coming at him with a gun. Again.

"Yeah." He breathed out, finding that he felt weak again, this time with relief. He pulled his hands away to wipe his forehead.

"I can get someone else."

He blinked, not quite understanding that. "What?"

Remi avoided his eyes. "If you don't feel safe, I can get someone else assigned to your case."

He almost laughed. "Don't be stupid, Archer."

"But—"

"I'm not the biggest fan of hitmen—hitwomen. But I was terrified because I thought she shot you—not because I don't feel safe."

She finally gave him a small smile. "Well, I'm the only agent prepared to deal with your insane work ethic."

"And I'm the only client willing to put up with

your language and bad attitude."

She laughed, and whatever leftover tension disappeared in the echo. Before he could overthink it, he pulled her into a hug, his hand tangling in her hair as he held her close. "I'm glad you're okay."

She laughed against his chest, both of her arms tight around him. "Same goes, pal."

They stood that way for a moment, finding comfort in the quiet. Finally, Remi sighed and pulled back. "Why don't you stay in here and get some rest while I go figure out how the hell Vanessa Masoft managed to get passed the metal detectors with the gun. I'm not leaving the building. There's water in the fridge if you need it."

"Okay."

Remi still hesitated. "If you need anything, call, and I'll be right back."

"I'm fine. Go."

She ran her hand over his arm, then vanished. Desmond heard her calling to someone as the door shut behind her.

He exhaled, looking around. There weren't many bright colors in the room. Mostly blues. A blue blanket on the bed. A blue dresser under the window. Knives splayed across the top of it, well used. Clothes spilled out of the closet; he recognized a few pairs of the garish colored socks she favored. His eyes drifted up, seeing pictures around the window.

He recognized a few faces. Gemma and Camille were in several. A girl who looked like Remi—her sister? An older gentleman between the two girls, his arms around both and a proud look in his eyes. And—

Him. The two of them actually. He was rolling his

eyes, amused, but trying not to show it. Remi was grinning, looking into the camera. It was a selfie she'd taken of them, on their way back from lunch last week, after the spicy food.

He didn't know what it meant, but he knew it was significant. The fact that she'd put up that picture, among all the people she called her friends and family. He had few friends. Rick and Ashley and…

Remi.

He stared at the picture for a long time.

****

Remi paused the video again, leaning forward. The computer chair creaked, the monitors of the research room casting a blue glow. Remi stared at the image, Vanessa raising the gun and aiming—

"If you didn't see it the first ten times," Camille began.

"Yeah, shut up."

Camille leaned back in her chair, stretching her arms above her head. "Why does this matter? You aren't free of him until you can prove who sent the messages. The one Thomas brought back couldn't tell us anything of importance. Delaney is still out there. What's one hitwoman?"

Remi spun her chair around when she heard a knock at the door. "Come in!"

Gemma walked in, passing out their mail as Remi answered. "Because, if she was an actual hitwoman, I'll eat Thomas' nasty overcoat. No way a person goes from committing petty crimes to hitwoman on the drop of a dime. And the payments Des was talking about don't match up to Masoft's bank account." She took a handful of mail that Gemma passed over to her. "I haven't been able to track the actual money because it gets sorted through three separate accounts. After that, it's distributed in prepaid cards. So that's unhelpful."

Camille took her mail from Gemma and turned her attention through that. Gemma paused in the doorway, looking at Remi with a faint frown.

"Got any advice?" Remi asked.

"Besides improving your attitude?" Gemma quipped, a delicate brow arched.

Remi couldn't help her grin as she skimmed through her mail. "Yeah."

"Consistent payments of over seven thousand dollars would make a significant change in someone's lifestyle. I'd stop trying to find where it went and start looking at possible recipients. We know it's someone involved with Delaney. Start there."

"How would one find the recipient if they're using cards not under their names?" Camille asked.

"There are other noticeable changes," Gemma said, flipping through the rest of the mail. "Dining out more often would result in cab fares or more spent on gas. Tailoring fees if they're buying more clothes. Increase in electrical bills for new electronics. A move to a bigger or better place, so recent changes in recurring bills like water or internet."

Remi stared at Gemma, her eyes narrowing. "What did you do before working here?"

"Many things."

With a laugh, Remi went through the rest of her mail.

Camille sat up straighter. "All right, so we'll begin with Delaney's lieutenants, looking for a change in lifestyle and—"

"Dammit," Remi whispered. She stared at a manilla envelope, her name on the front. No address, no return, no postage. Just her name.

"Remi?"

She didn't answer, but opened the envelope and reached in, grabbing a piece of paper and a photograph.

It was her and Desmond, today, after leaving the courthouse. Her arm stretched out in front of her, keeping people away from him. His eyes were cast down at the floor, but Remi was looking up, past the camera. She'd seen dozens of people taking pictures but hadn't really been paying attention. She'd been too focused on getting Desmond out of there to realize his stalker was right in front of them. She should've seen the bastard, but—

But she didn't.

"Oh, no," Camille said, having stood and looked over Remi's shoulder.

Gemma joined her and immediately began dialing the phone she carried with her at all times. "Thomas? It's Gemma. We need you in the research room."

"What's the letter say?" Camille asked in response to something Thomas asked.

Remi picked it up, scanning over the short lines.

He would've let the case go if it wasn't for you. This is your fault. His death will be on your hands. How long can you keep him safe? How long will you risk yourself?

How long until your luck runs out?

These bastards thought they could frighten her into giving up? Into talking Desmond into giving up? She tossed the papers to the side and stood.

Camille came to her feet, both hands raised to chest

level. "Remi…"

"Whatever you're thinking," Gemma began, her voice calm but tense. "it's probably a horrible idea."

"Probably." She grabbed the list of the known members of the Blackheart Gang and scanned it. A name popped: Bernie Glayes. A lower-level jerkoff with a sheet of priors for aggravated assault, drunk and disorderly, and breaking and entering, but a loyal dog for Delaney for several years. Someone who'd hear things. Know things.

Thomas walked in. "What's going—"

Remi pushed past him, stopping by the armory and loading up. She heard footsteps behind her, others rushing toward her— "Remi! Wait!"

"Miss Archer, please!"

She turned, only because they were now between her and the garage. She stared at Camille, Gemma, and Thomas blocking the hallway. The photo and letter were in Thomas's hand.

"I understand your frustration," he said, "but you can't do this."

"I'm going to go and have a little conversation with someone."

"Remi." Camille's eyes were pleading. "Don't."

"They threatened me. They almost shot Des, again. If you think I'm going to take this lying down—"

"What are you going to do?" Gemma asked. "Work your way through the ranks and kill them until someone gives you the answer you're looking for?"

"That's where I was gonna start, yeah."

"And if you never get an answer?"

Remi turned to Camille, and the other woman sighed in realization. "That's what you're hoping for."

"Either way, problem solved." Remi made to step around them. "Excuse me."

"Miss Archer," Thomas said, getting in her way. "Is this what you want to do? Go down the same road you decided to leave when you came to work here?"

"If it'll keep Des safe, then yes."

"So you'll go after them with guns; do you think they won't retaliate? More guns? More attacks? On Mr. Graves? His family? You? Us?"

"So I should back down?" Remi snapped, stepping into Thomas's face. "Sit back and let them keep trying while we flail around, getting nowhere but in their line of sight?"

"You do the job." Camille pushed between them, her hands hovering over Remi's arms. "You protect him, instead of leaving him behind. We've got your back, and we'll help you, but your job is to stand next to him."

Remi wavered, and she saw some of Thomas's tension fade. Only once had he stood between Remi and a goal. They both knew how the last time had gone. "I can't have another Anna," she warned them. "If that happens—"

"We've got leads. We need to push them through," Thomas said. "We have got a money trail, we've got names. We need to work the case."

"We'll keep him and his family safe," Gemma said.

Remi hesitated, then sighed, her shoulders sinking. "If something happens, you won't be able to stop me again."

"If something happens," Camille promised, "we'll be right behind you."

Remi nodded without her usual fervor, then held out her hand for the photo and letter. "I'll give them back. But I have to have a conversation."

Thomas handed them over but frowned. "Is it wise to tell him?"

"I don't keep secrets from him about the case. I'm not about to start now." She grabbed the papers and turned on her heel, back toward her room.

Hesitating outside of her door, she knocked, then stepped in. Desmond was at her desk, reading a book. Or pretending to read.

He took one look at her and put the book down. "Everything okay?"

"Everything's fine." Remi took a seat on the desk he was sitting at. "I just…shit." She rubbed her face, trying to find some ground here. "Okay, so I told you I'd be upfront about the case. That's the only reason I'm telling you about this. Because it doesn't change a thing, other than make me even more annoyed at these assholes. Okay? So I don't want you going all noble, because—"

"Archer."

She handed him the photo and letter, biting her cheek. He took them. Remi saw the moment he realized what it was, the tension returning to his neck and shoulders. He stared at the picture for a long time before going to the letter. He must have read it five times before he finally looked back up at her.

"They sent it to you?" His voice was flat, no inflection at all.

"Yeah. Here. Must have been by hand." She took them back from him, tossing them on the desk behind her. "Thomas is going to see if he can pull anything off the cameras or letters. We know they were at the courthouse, so we can narrow that down further."

He had yet to meet her eyes. Remi leaned down, forcing him to look at her. "This changes *nothing*. It doesn't matter. If you knew the number of threats I'd had—"

"But this one is because of me. If something happens—"

"It won't."

"But if it does—"

Remi cut him off again. "I know what my job is. I went into this with both eyes open. I chose this. I'm choosing to stay and protect you. I want to do this."

"Why?"

This brilliant moron. He didn't get it.

Remi leaned forward, grabbing his face between her hands and forcing him to look at her. "Because you are extraordinary, Graves. You are worth a million regular people. And if I have to break a thousand arms and spend the rest of my life making sure you're safe, I don't care, because you are worth it. I will never let anything happen to you so long as I can help it."

She felt his jaw jump beneath her fingers, felt his hand reach up and wrap around her wrist, squeezing. "Remi…" he breathed, and she had to rethink the intelligence of being quite this close to him.

His eyes darted downward, lingering on her lips, then back up. They were so close, and his hand was so warm against her wrist. His breath created goosebumps on her arms. His throat moved as he swallowed, meeting her eyes, and she shivered to see how dark his blue eyes had gotten. "Does that mean I'll get a refund for services?"

Remi laughed, the unexpected humor making it all the funnier. She rested her forehead on his for a heartbeat. Then she pulled away. She let go and put space between them before she did something stupid.

But it was too late.

****

Desmond stood by the judge's bench in the courthouse. The papers he'd come to grab were stacked on the prosecutor's table and waiting. His hands were in his pockets, as Remi spoke with a few cops she'd been unable to avoid. Though she'd clarified everything earlier, this seemed more like chatting among peers.

Desmond leaned on the podium, staring at Remi, but seeing her from this afternoon. She'd stood like a sentinel in the middle of the aisle, gun still up when he saw her the first time. In that single moment, he'd only felt fear. Now he thought of his high school literature class and the Valkyries of mythology. People associated them with brightness, gold, and bloodshed. Some of them collected the dead, some caused death, and some protected the lives of those dear to them.

Remi glanced back at him, a brief grin flashing. She turned back to the officers, clearly saying her goodbyes. Desmond didn't believe in the supernatural. But he wouldn't be surprised in the slightest if Remi was a real Valkyrie.

She walked toward him, eyes narrowing as she approached. "Everything okay?"

He didn't think she'd appreciate him waxing poetic about her. "Everything's fine."

"Let's get home," she said, grabbing some of his papers for him.

Desmond followed her, not particularly caring

where they went at this point. It was late by the time they arrived at his penthouse. The rain that had been threatening all morning finally arrived. It sprinkled down, creating a quiet hush of noise against the metal car. They didn't talk much on the ride there. Not that they didn't have tons to talk about, but they found some comfort in the quiet. When they got to his apartment, Remi parked on the sidewalk, turning off the car, but making no move to get out. She sighed, disturbing the quiet for the first time.

"Quite a day," Desmond said, still facing forward.

"No shit."

He chuckled without humor. "I've thanked you more than I've ever thanked anyone in my entire life. But I appear to owe you another one, for what you—"

"You don't need to thank me," she interrupted.

Desmond turned to her. "Remi, you killed someone for me today."

"Yeah." She finally looked at him. "So?"

He arched his brow. "After what you said about your past, how you didn't want to kill—"

"That's different." She sounded sure and calm. "Then, I killed on orders. This was protecting a friend. Vanessa had a gun, and she was shooting to kill. I have no regrets. And you never need to thank me for anything."

This was the second time they'd been close and quiet today. He was starting to enjoy these moments. Where Remi looked a little softer, a little brighter. She was still the same dangerous, foul-mouthed woman, but somehow more…attainable.

"I want…" He hesitated, unsure exactly what he was going to say. "I wanted to thank you for Ashley."

Remi rolled her eyes. "What did I just say?"

His laugh was brief but dispelled his awkwardness. "Fine."

Lightning flashed, lighting up the car. Remi's eyes turned toward the window, a softer smile on her lips. "I love the rain."

He followed her gaze. The gray clouds swirled above them, lightning bursting behind the whorls. All the while, a persistent mist of rain came down, making buildings shimmer and glass sparkle. Everything seemed a little brighter and cleaner.

When he looked back at her, she'd turned to him. The line between her eyes, the one she got when she was thinking hard about something, seemed to focus on him. Part of him wanted to ask what she was thinking about. The other part of him already knew because the same thoughts plagued him, and he wanted to see how this played out. So he remained silent and waited.

The line eased and faded, something decided. Remi's lips parted and she leaned forward—

And then her phone pinged.

He might have imagined the huff of annoyance from her because he'd made the same sound. She looked away from him, and whatever spell had been woven in the rain and the dark shattered. Desmond tried not to feel disappointed about it. And failed.

Remi read through whatever had arrived on her phone and rolled her eyes.

"What?" Desmond asked.

"Alec Singh," she said and sighed. "Camille and Farid's case has closed, so he wants to throw a party to celebrate."

"And you hate parties?"

Remi laughed. "No. But—" Desmond's phone pinged, and she gestured to it. "That'll be your invitation."

It was, for the coming Friday night. Black tie event. Desmond glanced at the list of guests, surprised to note that it was lengthy. "You don't want to go?"

"No, but I figured you—"

"I don't mind parties," he said, unsure what was behind her hesitation.

Remi smiled, pushing her gold hair back over her shoulder. "All right. Then do you want to go to the party?"

"With you?"

"Obviously. There are still a few psychopaths out there who are after you."

He was disappointed with her response. It was the clear answer, the only answer he should have expected, but…

But he remembered the warmth of her hands on his face this afternoon. He remembered how close she'd gotten, how honest she'd been with him, and he'd wondered…

He'd hoped.

So, doing his best to pull his courtroom bravado forward, he caught her eye. "Is this business or pleasure?"

The smile widened and softened. She tilted her head, not dropping his gaze. "Both. That okay?"

"Yes."

She laughed after a moment, then got out of the car, crossing to his side to walk him to the door. They didn't speak on the way up to his apartment. They didn't speak while she confirmed it was safe and empty.

They didn't speak as he walked her back to the door. They didn't speak at all until she was at the door. He stood in the doorway. "Goodnight."

She smiled, wagged her fingers. "'Night, Des."

He shut and locked the door behind her, listening for her to make her way toward the stairs.

Except she didn't.

He leaned his forehead against the door, knowing Remi was right on the other side. They both had to be thinking the same thing. His hand hesitated over the lock, and he imagined she had his key in her hand, waiting, and considering. What if...

Through the door, he heard an exhaled breath, then the sound of her footsteps moving toward the staircase. The whole incident had been nothing. A couple of seconds. But those seconds were the beginning of a real shift.

He stared at the counter where his phone rested, recalling the party invitation. He and Remi attending a black-tie party together, huh?

He'd have to deliver.

Chapter Eight

Desmond paused in his normal morning routine when the phone he'd tossed on the bathroom counter started to ring. After glancing at the picture, he answered. "Ashley. I left you three messages. What happened?"

"Not everyone has your level of security with a 'get out of the drama free' card." He heard the sound of her ancient coffee maker in the background. "They kept me there for a while. Samara was able to get them to spring me and told you were okay, but I didn't get home 'til late." A pause and Ashley's acerbic tone faded. "Are you okay?"

"I am." He carried the phone into the kitchen while he packed his briefcase. "Are you?"

"Of course. Your girl shot her dead. No worries for any of the rest of us now."

He paused in shutting his briefcase. *His girl.*

"You going to this Alec person's party?"

"They invited you, too?" he asked, fixing his tie.

"Yeah, and I'm going. Samara said they're pretty kickass. And there's an open bar."

He chuckled. "Yeah. I'll be there. Rick is on the list, too."

"Yeah, he called. Mind if I take the car, then?"

"Bring it back in one piece the next day."

"Obviously," Ashley said. "Guess I'll see you

Friday night. Glad you're not dead or anything."

"Thanks," he drawled.

"Tell Remi I say hi."

That was too specific to be innocent. "What's that supposed to mean?"

"Defensive, big brother?"

"Annoying, little sister?" He hefted the strap of his briefcase over one shoulder and headed to the door, switching the phone back to private.

"Hey, she's hot. And kicks ass. I don't blame you."

He walked down the stairs, dropping his voice. "We are not discussing this."

"So there's something to discuss?"

"Goodbye, Ashley," Desmond said, reaching the landing.

"Bye, Romeo."

He hung up before she could start in on him again, shoving the phone in his pocket. Moments later a text came through. With an irritated sigh, he pulled out the phone again, reading it while walking down the stairs. It was from Remi.

—Here.—

He found that he was smiling, even as another one came from his sister.

—Have a good day, loverboy.—

With another roll of his eyes, he reached the lobby and nodded to Peter, seeing Remi outside the door. She smiled as he arrived, the two of them falling into step together.

"Hey," she said, handing him a coffee. "How'd you sleep?"

"Well. You?"

"Shitty." She took a long sip from her cup. "They

found where Masoft was staying."

"And?"

She sighed, stepping a little nearer and lowering her voice. "Lots of firepower. Same paper as the letters. Cameras." She stopped, then looked up at him. "A fuck-ton of pictures of you, Ashley and me."

He frowned, sipping his drink. "So, either she was the mastermind behind all this, and missed her shot at the courthouse…"

"Or someone's going through a lot of effort to make it look like she was. But they suck at it," she added. "She had approval to carry a weapon into the building, which makes no sense. I have paperwork that allows it because of my job. No one in their right mind would sign off on her."

"You underestimate how much the police dislike me, Archer."

There was a flash of anger on Remi's face, then she continued. "The last letter and picture came after she was dead. The paper was there, but it was every sheet of a five hundred ream package. We counted. The cameras were completely clean—not even Alec could get anything off of it. And the guns there, they matched—"

She cut herself off, shaking her head. They waited for the light to change so they could cross the street, traffic light this morning. "They matched the kind that hit you, but the striations from the bullets are different."

"Sounds like you had a busy night."

She snorted, stopping outside his building. "This case is so backward. Should be a high-functioning psychopath of some kind, but we get a shitty crook. She's got all the right kinds of tools, but not exact. She somehow shot her motivation and ended up dead herself. It doesn't make sense." She ran her fingers through her hair, her eyes looking everywhere.

"We'll figure it out." Neither of his hands was free, but he wished they were.

Remi's mouth quirked up as she met his eyes. "Of course we will, but it's irritating the hell out of me in the meantime."

He chuckled, her easy confidence easing any tension or discomfort from this case. This horrible, terrifying case, which part of him wasn't even annoyed about. It had brought him Remi.

"I'll see you at lunch," she said. "You've gotta finish Jesse Randall's disaster of a case."

"I should work through lunch—"

"Bull. We didn't have dinner last night. You need to eat." Her tone left no room for argument, and he didn't want to. Before Remi, skipping lunch was a normal occurrence. Now, it was a highlight of his day. "I wanna try that Ethiopian place on Cedar."

"Fine." He failed to keep his tone neutral. "See you later."

She winked at him. "Not if I see you first."

She watched until he got inside, waving at him as he looked back. He went up to his office and unpacked his briefcase, his mind turning on several things unrelated to work.

He was with Remi that Masoft couldn't have been the mastermind behind it all. It was clear someone wanted them to think so, though. That must mean they were getting close to discovering who, and he'd accused Delaney that very day. Moments before Masoft walked in.

It would have to be someone who knew him and his priorities, not that those weren't easy enough to discern. He spent his time with work, Rick, and Ashley. It would be easy to figure out what mattered to him.

Remi hadn't been subtle with Delaney at the funeral, and he knew who she was. Getting a letter delivered to her work wasn't surprising.

Everything pointed to Delaney, but Remi was right, the timing didn't work out.

Sagging into his chair, Desmond rubbed his temples. Then he sighed, straightening and opening up his inbox. The email from Alec sat near the top, and Desmond RSVP'd while he was still thinking of it. At least that was something to look forward to.

****

Remi dropped Desmond off that night, making sure he locked up behind her. They'd ordered pizza for dinner. Actually, Remi had ordered it after Desmond made a fuss over eating without utensils at lunch. She'd teased him, grabbing a pizza on the way back for dinner. Despite his complaints that it was cleaner, she forced him not to use a fork and knife.

She made a mental note to pick up donuts in the morning and find a hotdog place near his work for lunch tomorrow.

The drive back to Exceptional Security was quiet. She didn't even turn on music, still trying to churn over the case and coming up empty. It didn't make sense. No matter which way she turned it, Delaney was the best suspect and Masoft was guilty. But neither of them fit both the timing or the motive.

She parked in the garage, turning off the car and sitting for a few minutes. Rubbing at her temples, she tried to will away the migraine that had been present ever since this morning. She'd been getting hourly updates from Alec and Farid, and Camille checked in often, but no one had anything new. None of Delaney's people had moved recently, nor had any significant changes in behavior. But it had to be one of them.

She walked up to the lobby, found Gemma behind the desk, dressed to the nines, per usual. The glass looked black in the dark, and Remi's quiet footsteps echoed in the silence. She walked past the desk, then paused. An insignificant but irritating thought kept her from going to her room.

She froze until the other woman sighed. "Can I help you, Miss Archer?"

Remi turned back, plucking at her sleeve. "Uh, this party Alec's throwing."

"Yes?" Gemma didn't turn, still focused on her computer.

"Is it…you know?"

"We vetted all attendees and will have the usual party security measures."

"No." Remi shifted, knowing that it would be as safe as possible. "I meant…it's like, fancy, right?"

That made Gemma turn, the chair swiveling toward her as she sat back and eyed Remi. "Yes. Black tie."

"So that's like, dresses and stuff?"

Gemma's brow furrowed. "That would be correct."

Remi chewed on her lip. "So, do you know where…I mean, I haven't exactly had a reason to buy crap like that. And since you're always put together—"

Gemma stood, the chair rolling back a few inches. "Miss Archer, are you asking me to help you pick out a dress?"

"I…yes?"

Gemma grinned. "I would love to."

"Great. Thanks."

"You'll be attending with Mr. Graves?" Gemma asked, brow arching.

"Yeah, I'll bring him here after work. Leaves him about an hour or so to get his shit ready, and that's if we leave his work on time."

"Lovely." Gemma's eyes seemed lost in thought. "Well, we should get started."

"Right now?" Remi asked. "But it's late. Everything's closed."

Gemma laughed, locking the computer and putting it on night-mode. The doors now only allowed entrance with a key card and passcode. "We're not going out."

She walked past Remi down the back stairs to their basement level. This floor housed storage rooms, as well as the mainframe. Remi was familiar with this floor, having dealt with the mainframe a few times. But she'd never ventured into the door next to it, labeled "Supplies."

Gemma pushed open the door, and Remi paused on the threshold, looking at the massive closet of clothes. Remi's eyes widened as she stepped inside. "What the hell?"

"Every outfit used for a mission or purchased with company money." Gemma sounded smug. "And I know a very talented seamstress who would be able to help you with alterations. So have at it. Ball gowns are near the back, left-hand side. I'll join you in a few moments. There's a changing room in the back. Try some on, see what you like."

With that, Gemma turned and left, the door

propped open behind her and her heels clicking away. Reminding herself that she'd asked for this, Remi walked back to the corner. Passing formal men's suits, clothing for extreme weather, and armor-reinforced jackets, she finally found a line of ball gowns.

She immediately decided she hated the ones that were tight around the legs. She needed mobility of movement, party or not. Something flowy. A red one caught her eyes, with lace on the sides. And a green one that was shorter on one side. A blue one that was simple and satin. A fourth dress made her pause, but she didn't grab it. Stepping into the changing room, she got dressed in the red one. A few curious wrigglings of her arms helped her zip it up. She opened up the dressing room door to look at the mirror outside.

"That's a little…bold."

Remi turned, seeing Camille, Samara, and Gemma all behind her.

"Yeah." Samara perched on a pile of shoes, appraising her. "That's a dress that says someone is gonna get lucky." She eyed the ones Remi had already picked. "Try the blue one. That looks promising."

"I didn't bring you here to accost her," Gemma said.

"No, it's fine. Not feeling this one." Remi stripped out of it and grabbed the blue one. Camille came up and helped her fix the satin straps. When she deemed it ready, Camille stepped back.

Gemma was smiling. "I like this one."

"It's pretty," was Samara's only comment.

Remi spun. She liked the color, and it was okay, but…

"Try the green one."

Once again, Remi stripped and pulled on the next one. This was okay. The fit was better. The color was fine. She left it on, but her eyes drifted to the rack.

"Something else caught your eye?" Gemma asked.

She shrugged, wandering back over to the rack and grabbing the dress she'd passed over earlier. She went to the changing room, dropping the green one on the floor and pulling the new one over her head. It was simple—with wrapped straps that led to a low, very low-cut back. The front was modest enough, with a flowy diaphanous skirt. She knew before she stepped out that this was the one.

Camille's eyes went wide as soon as Remi appeared. "Oh, wow."

Samara grinned. "Yes."

"Excellent choice," Gemma said.

"Thanks." She took another moment, then got changed. Hanging up the other ones, she put the one she chose over her arm.

Gemma took it from her. "I'll get this dry cleaned for you and have it in your room for Friday. You'll look beautiful."

"And you can fit an arsenal beneath that skirt." Samara tossed a wink at her.

Remi grinned. "Damn straight."

"Gonna be one hell of a party," Camille said, heading toward the door.

Remi's smile stayed in place until all the others turned to leave. As she trailed behind the women, the smile faded.

Yes, sir. One hell of a party.

****

On Friday night, Desmond straightened his cuffs.

Fixing the cufflinks Ashley had gotten him for Christmas, he used the mirror in Remi's room to check how he looked. Camille and Gemma had appeared shortly after he and Remi had arrived. Despite Remi's eye-rolling, they absconded with her. He'd laughed at her expression, then proceeded to get ready.

This wasn't a suit he wore often. The last time, he'd been receiving an award from his bureau for distinguished service, code for the most convictions in a year. Still, it had been a fancy to-do, and this was the suit he'd purchased for it. He rarely wore tuxes. The lines of a suit were better for him, the midnight blue of the fabric made his figure more intimidating. Not that it would matter tonight with Remi running around—but it made him feel more confident. It was best suited for special occasions, which this was.

He couldn't deny a sense of anticipation for tonight, as there always was on the night of a big event. He tried not to read into it, but ever since Monday, there had been so many more brief touches from Remi. She played them off as unintentional or casual, but it felt like more. She lingered after dropping him off at home, sometimes the two of them having a drink before she left. They chatted about her childhood abroad or his early years in the firm. What it was like to have siblings. Her tumultuous friendship with Thomas and his complicated history with Rick.

Even now, getting ready gave off the juvenile excitement of prom. He hadn't attended his, and Remi joked about how the seniors kicked her out of hers. It was stupid and exhilarating, and Desmond couldn't help but wonder what might happen if this wasn't part of her job. If this evening had been for pleasure.

But it wasn't. He straightened his perfect tie, knowing that Remi would be working tonight. He wouldn't begrudge her for it. She was doing it because she cared, not because he was her responsibility or job. Still, he wondered what could happen if she was his date. If there weren't any stalkers or hitmen or gangs, and if it was just the two of them.

He checked his appearance in the mirror once more, glancing at the picture of him and Remi before leaving. In the hallway, Camille was leaving her room. She had dressed for the part as well, in a vibrant maroon dress that hugged her figure and a thick, gold necklace. She looked over at him as he approached and smiled. "You look rather dashing."

He grinned, nodding his head. "And still nowhere near as good as you."

Camille laughed. "Remi was right, you've got a way with words. She's about done. See you up there."

Desmond watched her go, leaning against the wall opposite her door. He checked his watch, the silver tracking bracelet knocking against it. Five minutes went by without any sign of her.

Looking forward to a drink, he knocked on the door. "If you take much longer, Rick's going to have drained the place dry."

He heard her laugh. "True. One second."

He didn't have time to step back as she opened the door, and both of them froze, a few inches between them. Even if Desmond hadn't been surprised, he still couldn't have moved away.

Remi's hair was loose but curled over one shoulder. She was closer to his eye level, heels hidden by the hem of her dress, but it was the dress—

It wasn't the delicate straps or the silky material. It wasn't the way it fit her perfectly, or how the ephemeral skirt fell in such a way that it always appeared to be moving. It wasn't how it revealed so much and not *enough*—

It was the color. Pure, simple white.

He realized he'd stared too long when she shifted, her cheeks turning pink. "Is it okay?"

"Yes." His word sounded abrupt. "Yes, you look…" He trailed off, his infamous way with words becoming snarled and convoluted when it came to her. "You look good in white."

She smirked, red lips twisting into a familiar smile. "Thanks, hotshot. You earn the name in that suit. Well done."

He chuckled. "Thanks. Have to keep up with you."

"You think I'm hot?" She echoed him from what felt like years ago. How had it just been a few weeks?

"That's not what I said." Desmond waited until she looked behind her to shut the door. "But yes, I do."

She looked back at him, smiling again. "Come on, let's get to that bar."

Letting her take the lead, per usual, Desmond stuttered when he caught sight of the back of the dress. Or rather, the lack of. Miles of pale skin stretched from her shoulders to the small of her back. His hand immediately clenched into a fist so as not to try and touch her. If he started, he may not stop.

Glancing back, she quirked her brow. "You coming?"

Jesus, she'd be the death of him.

But what a way to go…

****

The elevator ride was quiet and tense for Remi. Desmond's reaction to her appearance had been what she'd been hoping for, even if she tried not to consider it. What she hadn't expected had been the turnabout.

She knew he wore suits. Expensive, fancy fucking suits day in and day out. But something about this one made her skin burn. Maybe it was the fit over the shoulders that made them seem wider. Or the contrast of the striped shirt—should it be that tight?—against the deep cobalt of the jacket. Or that bow tie that lay so straight and begged for her to mess it up. Or—

No. It was because it was Desmond.

Whatever the reason, she had to concentrate not to look at him the entire ride up to the top floor. The hand farthest from him fidgeted with the blade hidden on her thigh. Rarely did she curse her focus, but she could feel Desmond standing close to her. His heady cologne seemed to fill the air. The sound of his measured breaths and the near-silent tick of his watch plucked her nerves. She made the mistake of looking over before the elevator opened.

His darkened blue eyes were on her, staring, and she couldn't look away. She licked her suddenly dry lips—

The door dinged open.

They both looked away, the spell interrupted by music and conversation. Remi, forcing a smile, stepped out of the elevator. Taking in a breath of air that wasn't flavored with Desmond, her head cleared. Spotting the bar, she led the way, taking in the sights and making sure Desmond was nearby at all times.

Alec had outdone himself. The top floor was mostly bulletproof windows that got too much sun during the day. Tonight, though, it led to an amazing view of the city. Blue and red balloons gathered in clusters around the room, and streamers hung from the ceiling. A young man serenaded the guests, a full band backing him. Not so loud as to drown out conversation, but enough for the dancers in the center of the room. Waiters carried flutes of champagne and finger foods, offering them to everyone. The wide-open patio doors let out to a garden lit up with fairy lights and provided fresh, cool air.

It was pretty fantastic.

Remi smiled at Samara and Camille from across the room, waving at them through the crowd of people. She recognized most of them as politicians, lawyers, and some high-ranking law enforcement. Though Gemma had vetted each of them, Remi remained vigilant.

"Hey, guys!"

Remi braced herself, turning to see Alec Singh. His boyish looks made it hard to believe he was the head of Singh Technology. His grin was only matched by his enthusiasm, and Remi had to keep reminding herself that he meant well.

"Hey, Alec." She gave him a brief hug because that's what one did with Alec. "Great party."

"Thanks. I'm glad you could make it." He looked at Desmond. "Mr. Graves, I've followed your cases for several years. I have to say, you are the most positive force for change in this city."

Desmond seemed a little taken aback. "Thanks. That means a lot, especially from someone who's changing the world of technology."

He laughed without arrogance, just exuberance. "I

know. Wait until you see what we're working on next. But what I wanted to say was, do you want to meet for lunch sometime when all this quiets down? I'd love to pick your brain on the prison system and see what changes we could make. I want to focus on the software we use there, along with a few ideas I've got for a reliable polygraph."

Remi laughed as Desmond stared at Alec for a moment, trying to catch up with the genius's train of thought. "Yeah, sure, sounds good."

"Wonderful! Now, enjoy the party. People need to start dancing soon." He threw finger guns at the two of them. "See you later."

Desmond stared after him for a long moment. "What just happened?"

Remi laughed, bumping into his shoulder. "That's Alec. Now you see what I meant when I said we couldn't get rid of him. You talked to him for two seconds and now have a lunch meeting."

He shook his head. "Let's get those drinks. I need one after—"

"Hey, Desi. You sure pick the swankiest of parties."

Remi turned, seeing Ashley behind them.

Desmond smiled, leaning down to kiss his sister's cheek. "You look great."

She did, in her bold red dress. Her makeup and hair were on point, too. Remi smiled at her. "Nice to see you again."

"Yeah, you too," Ashley said. "Did you get to ride in the fancy secret elevator? All us plebes had to use the stairs outside."

Desmond laughed. "Yes, we did."

Ashley glanced at Remi, her smile got a little sharper. She looked at Desmond. "Mind if I steal your date for a sec?"

Remi smiled when Desmond glanced at her, easing his confusion. "I'll find you, no worries."

"See you at the bar."

Remi watched him go, then looked at Ashley. The smile was replaced by irritation and anger in her eyes. "What the hell are you doing? Masoft almost put a bullet in him."

"I know. But she didn't—"

"You need to get your head out of your ass and look out for my brother. If you weren't half in love with him—"

"I am *not* half in—"

"Fully then, whatever." Ashley snapped. "You're supposed to protect him."

"I am protecting him," Remi said, ignoring the other comment.

"You let her get *within feet* of him."

Remi stepped in a little closer. "Look, I'm doing everything I can to protect Desmond. Whatever you think my feelings are, they aren't going to get in the way of the job."

Ashley nodded over Remi's shoulder. "And is this only a job?"

Remi turned and caught sight of Desmond at the edge of the bar. His eyes swept across the dance floor, a tumbler in his hand. Samara was next to him, and the two of them were chatting about something that made Samara laugh. His eyes caught hers; he gave her a soft smile.

Remi couldn't help but return it. She held back her

flinch when Ashley scoffed. "I knew it. Get it under control," she hissed. "Or I'll find someone who can." She turned on her heel and walked away, disappearing between other guests.

Remi watched her go, taking a minute to gather her composure. She told herself that Ashley wasn't right. Her emotions didn't make her bad at her job. This job was bad and made no sense, but part of her wondered if Ashley had a point. If Remi wasn't so caught up in him, would she have seen the photographer outside the courthouse...?

She exhaled, then turned and walked toward the bar. Desmond caught her approach, ordering something for her. She slid into the seat next to him, taking the glass from the bartender with thanks.

Desmond watched her for a moment, that concerned line appearing between his eyes. "Everything okay?"

"Everything's fine."

He leaned closer, his hand lifting toward her arm. "You sure?"

She was saved from answering when Rick appeared. Somewhere, he'd managed to scrounge up slacks, a shirt broad enough to cover his chest, and a decent vest. No jacket and the sleeves were rolled up, but he'd made an effort.

"Hey," he rumbled, holding up a finger to the bartender. Clearly familiar with Rick, the bartender pulled out a bottle and a much larger glass than Remi had.

"Looking good, Rick," Remi said.

He grunted, looking her up and down. "Nice."

Remi laughed, taking it as a compliment. "What're

you drinking?"

"Everything," muttered the bartender.

Rick leaned against the bar, looking out over the party. "Got a nice place. And you do some decent work." He took a deep swig of his drink and put the glass down, looking at Remi. "You guys hiring?"

Desmond shot a glance at Remi, the smile both annoyed and unsurprised. Remi shrugged. "We're always looking for new people. Means you have to work with a team, though."

"If you can manage, I'll be fine." Rick's eyes cut over to her.

Remi agreed with a smile. "I'll give Thomas your number. We'll see what we can do."

With that, Rick pushed off the bar and left, leaving Remi under Desmond's gaze.

"You stole my investigator," he muttered.

"I didn't do anything. Besides, all that means is that you'll have to hang out here. Is that so bad?" she asked before she could stop herself.

Desmond stared at her for several heartbeats. "No, it's not."

The music was good, so it was no surprise when Ashley came bouncing up. She had a polite smile for Remi, then asked Desmond, "Wanna dance?"

He hesitated, but like the funeral, he did it for Ashley. Rolling his eyes as he left, the two of them went to the dance floor. He guided her rather well for someone who seemed to dislike dancing. Remi sat back in her seat and sipped her drink, keeping her eyes open.

"I'm surprised not to see you on the dance floor."

Remi didn't flinch, having heard Thomas's characteristic footsteps. "I'm on the clock."

"No rest for the wicked, huh?" Thomas took the seat next to her.

"Is that why you always look exhausted?"

"I thought that would have been obvious."

He cleaned up well, their boss. Not as nice as some, but nice enough. Remi caught several men and women casting glances over at him.

"How have you been holding up?" he asked.

"Fine. Just want to figure this disaster out." Remi drained her glass.

"You seem to be working well with Mr. Graves." Remi glanced over at Thomas at the comment, but he continued. "I was thinking of asking him to remain on retainer."

"How so?"

Thomas chuckled. "You and I both know the work we do isn't always above board. The company's doled out a hefty sum to keep several of our clients and associates out of prison." He looked pointedly at her. "It would be helpful to have a lawyer such as Mr. Graves to give us some guidance."

"I could see that," she said, ordering another.

"Do you have an objection?"

Remi shook her head. "No. Not at all. He's a great lawyer. A good man. We'd be lucky to have him."

"As he's lucky to have us," Thomas added.

Remi cut her eyes at him, but he was looking at the dance floor. He stood. "Enjoy the party." Then he walked off, in that infuriating, enigmatic way of his.

Remi glared after him, seeing Samara dragging a young man onto the dance floor. Camille and Rick were in one corner, both of them putting back several large glasses. Farid Nassar and Alec debated something that involved three shrimp cocktails as props. Gemma stalked across the floor and interrupted Thomas's conversation. He looked startled before he grinned and offered her his arm, leading her to the dance floor. They passed right by Ashley and Desmond, who spun in such a way that Desmond was able to wink at Remi across the room.

She smiled, finishing her drink. If it weren't for the stalker, this might be one of the best nights of her life.

As it was, stalkers and potential murder were pretty regular for her, so it was close to being perfect. She caught Desmond's eyes again and smiled, warmth unrelated to the alcohol filling her.

****

Desmond finally escaped from Farid and Alec. How there could be two people as enthusiastic as Alec, he'd never know.

"Remember, Desmond. Thursday nights. You'll love it," Farid promised as he walked away.

As strange as it was, Desmond was intrigued. Farid wanted him to join his game nights with Alec, Thomas, and Samara. He'd also been roped into lunch with Alec and a business meeting with Thomas after his case closed. He couldn't remember the last time he had a standing appointment with anyone other than a client, Rick, or Ashley.

Still, as much as he enjoyed the oddity, he found himself searching the room for one person. He'd been dragged into one conversation after another. He'd danced with Ashley, Camille, and even Gemma twice. It was a little much. Especially when all he wanted to do was be with—

"Get enlisted into their game night?"

Desmond turned, unsurprised that Remi had managed to catch him unaware. His breath seemed to catch all over again at her outfit. "Apparently."

"They're a good bunch. I've been a couple of times," she admitted. "It was more fun than I thought it'd be."

"I'll admit, I'm interested." He smiled, taking the glass she offered. "Thanks."

"Anytime, hotshot."

They stood in silence for a moment, the music shifting to something a little slower and softer.

"Haven't seen you dancing." He looked down at her. He'd noticed several people asking, but she'd said no to them. Much to his relief.

Remi smiled, not looking at him. "I'm also working, remember?"

"Thought this was business and pleasure."

"It is. But I can't go dance if it means leaving you here—"

"Then dance with me."

She hesitated upon looking up at him, one of the first times he'd seen her hesitate with anything. The expression on her face was almost cautious for a moment. But it vanished, replaced with a grin. "Sure."

Part of him was surprised when she said yes. But he took her hand and led her onto the dance floor. Keeping hold of her, he spun her around, placing his other hand along the small of her back. He'd forgotten for a moment about the dress, and he had to take a breath as his fingers touched bare skin.

The piano picked up, the delicate notes cutting through the conversation. They began swaying, a comfortable distance between the two of them. He found his gaze wandering over the crowd, looking everywhere but the woman in his arms, but he couldn't keep that up. Not for long.

He glanced down, seeing Remi looking up at him. The two of them stayed there for a moment, and he wasn't certain who moved first. That friendly distance vanished, and he pulled her closer or she stepped in. There they swayed, cheek to cheek, hip to hip, chest to chest.

It had been two weeks, and he couldn't imagine his life without her in it.

Desmond took a breath, the smell of metal and vanilla emanating from her skin. He smiled to himself, recalling the donuts she'd brought him the other morning, that wicked grin on her face. She challenged him in everything: his work habits, his eating habits, his negative thoughts. She challenged him to be better in every way.

He recalled her face as she stole a bite of his Indian food, the spice shocking her, and her laughter afterward. The only woman he'd ever known who could take on an armed woman and a mobster yet flinch at the sight of vindaloo. That openness she had with him about everything she thought and felt.

Her tiny smile as she played the piano in his living room. The easy familiarity she had in his home and the sight of his picture in hers. They both belonged somewhere, even if it wasn't so much a place, as it was a person. Each other.

Remi turned her head to rest her cheek against his chest. Desmond's quiet, guarded heart gave a little stutter as his entire world shifted.

****

Remi sighed, comfort sliding into her bloodstream like a morphine drip. She was the protector in this arrangement, but every day it felt like it was a little more the reverse. Desmond was like a barrier between her and the horrible things they faced. Not because they were ignoring it, but because he made it clear they were in this together.

A hum from his chest vibrated beneath her cheek and she smiled. She remembered how he hummed the same chorus of a song they'd heard from a passing car for two days straight. Little snippets of music got stuck in his head and he shared with everyone.

She thought about that annoyed expression he gave her every time she did something she shouldn't. The one that wasn't truly annoyed but pretending to be for the sake of saving face. The one he gave when she told people what he wanted to say but wouldn't. The one when she threatened Delaney before he'd laughed in the car.

His infuriating way of letting his work consume him, which wasn't infuriating enough. She knew he just cared that much about putting criminals away, so no one would have to suffer as he had. How he let people believe the worst of him. How sometimes he thought he deserved it. How she wanted to convince him that he was worth more.

The comfort she felt in his home, the day he'd worn a sweater. How she'd lounged on his couch, and they talked about the case and his family, and ate Chinese food and made a mess. How it wasn't home, not like the one she'd grown up in with her sister, but it could be. Because it had him in it.

She remembered his laugh and the way Rick had

glanced at her in surprise tonight. She'd managed to draw it out of him, and the pride she felt for making him laugh when no one else seemed to. The idea that she wanted to make him laugh every day.

And damn, maybe the two of them were inevitable. She hadn't anticipated it to happen so quickly, and without concern or panic, but it was *Desmond.*

Jesus, she was so screwed.

Still, that didn't stop her from pressing a little bit closer. Desmond's hand rested at the small of her back, and she felt like her skin was on fire. Her breathing hitched and she closed her eyes. She could have this moment before they went back to stalkers and murderers.

"Remi." Desmond's voice murmured in her ear.

She looked up, finding his darkened eyes fixed on her. The expression on his face was one she hadn't seen before. Hopeful anticipation, tempered beneath his courtroom mask. But she could see his thoughts mirroring hers.

Before either of them said anything more, the song ended, and they stepped back from one another. Remi's skin felt cold in the absence of his hands. Applause filled the room as the singer bowed, and Remi and Desmond joined in, not looking at one another. They walked toward the edge of the dance floor. A new song began before Remi found the courage to look him in the eye. Nothing had happened, but everything had changed in those two minutes.

Desmond was still looking at her, his expression unchanged from what it had been. She smiled and he seemed to let go of his restraint, taking her hand. "I think I've had enough dancing for tonight."

Remi shivered. "Party's winding down anyway."

It was true, crowds were milling around, heading downstairs to the parking lot. They joined the mob, neither of them speaking. With every brush of his hand against her arm, Remi found it harder and harder to maintain normalcy.

They reached the parking lot, weaving through the cars. Desmond's hand found hers, their fingers intertwining as if they'd done this a thousand times before. Remi smiled to herself, this simple thing making her traitorous heart flip in her chest.

When she heard the beep, she looked up, but it was too late to do anything but watch as the car in front of them exploded.

Chapter Nine

Desmond remembered a long-ago car accident. He was in either fifth or sixth grade and his mother had driven him and Ashley to school. It was one of her bad days, and Desmond recalled trying to convince her to let them walk to school. But it was cold, and the sky was still dark, so she'd insisted, though it took all her effort to get out of bed.

They were close to the school when they hit a patch of black ice. His mother never saw it. They slid into an intersection and were T-boned by an oncoming sedan. The force of the crash spun their car onto the median with a metallic shriek.

He remembered the doctors who poked and prodded afterward—then the visits from the Department of Child Services right there in the hospital. If he tried, he could occasionally bring back the firefighters cutting him and Ashley out of their seatbelts, then the ambulance ride to the hospital. He remembered screaming from the hideous pain, then a cottoned pressure that surrounded him, keeping him from feeling his injuries. Then the sweet numbness before the pain crept in all over again.

Like now, if he tried, he only heard muffled screams. He felt that thick pressure enclose him. But it hadn't been raining that day near his school, so why did he feel water now…?

He forced his eyes open; that action brought new pain front and center. Ashes floating in a cloud around him mixed with the pouring rain. It wasn't enough to smother the fire that burned several yards away, but it drowned a few of the smaller ones.

Coughing, he tried to sit up, but a firm hand on his shoulder kept him down. Craning his neck, he found Remi, gun in hand, kneeling at his side.

"Don't move, not yet," she said, her voice hoarse. There were streaks on the white dress. Ashes and something red. "How does your neck feel? Your head?"

"I'm fine," he croaked.

She looked at him closely and he saw how pale she was, even beneath the cover of soot on her face. "Des, a concussion—"

"I know what a concussion feels like, Archer." He pushed her arm away and leaned up on one elbow. "What happened?"

"Car bomb."

People surrounded them. Some wailed; others cried. Sirens sounded in the distance. "Ashley? Rick?" he asked.

"I don't know."

He made to stand up, but she grabbed his arm, exerting enough pressure to keep him in place. "That was our damn car, Graves. I have to get you out of here."

"Ashley is—"

"Samara is on it. Rick will be fine, but I need to get you away from here."

He wanted to argue, but Remi finally looked him in the eye. "Please."

Guilt forced him to relent. "Fine."

She stood, and he noticed a faint wince. His chest constricted even further. "Remi—"

"Stay close and stay down."

He did, hovering next to her. The ringing in his ears was fading, leaving behind the sound of screams, and someone crying. There were shouts, trying to establish order in the chaos, but it wasn't working yet.

"Why don't we go back inside?" he asked, seeing where she was leading him.

"Because the bomb was here." Her voice was emotionless. "It wasn't on the car before we got here, meaning it was put on after. That means—"

"It was someone at the party."

Remi gave him a brief nod. She unlocked the bag on the back of a motorcycle, handing him a jacket. "Might be a bit tight, but it's kevlar. And here." She passed him a helmet. "Put it on."

"Where's yours?"

She ignored him. "Hurry up." She grabbed her phone, from where Desmond had no idea, and made a call. "Thomas, it's me. I'm getting Graves out of the area and back to his place. I'll need someone to secure it as soon as possible. I've got my bag. Get back to me as soon as you can."

After he put the helmet on, she nodded and got onto the bike. "Come on."

He did, and his hands hovered, not sure what to do. "Hold on."

Beneath him the bike lurched; he grabbed her waist. Remi peeled out of the parking lot and onto the city streets. Behind him, as the screams rose, Desmond couldn't help but wonder who they were abandoning.

****

Cold rain stung her face as Remi sped them through the city. She took side streets, backtracking until her fingers froze and her teeth chattered. Then she did it for a little bit longer before approaching Desmond's apartment building.

How the hell did she not see this coming?

She parked in the back of his building, helped him off the bike, then find his bearings. She checked her phone, seeing a text from Thomas.

—Don't know how this happened yet. Your car, remote detonated. Alec, Camille, and Farid accounted for. Still waiting on the others.—

She texted back, not wanting to worry Desmond yet.

—The second you have word on Rick and Ashley, call.—

—Of course. Stay safe.—

Remi grabbed the bag from the other side of her bike. She took the helmet from Desmond but gestured for him to leave the jacket on. He did, following her up the stairwell to his apartment. She wasn't going to risk the elevator, not tonight. Unlocking his door with her key, she had him wait in the kitchen while she did a thorough sweep of the entire apartment. It was clean.

Locking the door behind them, Remi breathed a sigh of relief. Then she turned to Desmond. "Are you okay?"

He took off the jacket, with a sharp look. "Is there any word on Ashley and Rick?"

She didn't say anything.

"Then I'm not okay." He hung her jacket over the back of a chair. "If it wasn't for me—"

"No." Remi interrupted him, stepping closer.

"Don't even start. This isn't your fault. This is the fault of some psychopath. You aren't why this is happening—they are. None of this is on you."

He didn't answer but lifted his eyes.

"Now, are you okay?" she asked again, putting her hand on his arm and trying to see any point of injury.

He shifted a little, moving his shoulders and arms. "I'm fine."

She glared at him.

"Really, Remi. Sore, but I'm okay. You?"

"I'm fine."

"You're bleeding."

She looked down, seeing red spots on her dress. Suppressing an unreasonable sense of sorrow over the dress, she ran a hand over the spots. "Just gravel. It's fine."

If it wasn't the blood that ruined it, the rain would have. They were both soaked through, the rain picking up and sliding down in great sheets over the windows. Lightning crackled in the distance, and she imagined she saw a faint fire. She took a step toward the glass, her gaze dropping to the sidewalk. The rain forced people inside and out of the way. She didn't see anyone outside, so no immediate danger.

"If you want," she said, "you can take a shower. I'll wait for Thomas to call."

"You're not leaving?"

Remi shook her head. "I can't. One, the danger to you is still there. Two, if they've attacked us once, they might do it again. I can't risk getting stuck in transit or in another shitstorm like what happened." She turned to him. "So, I guess we're roomies for a bit." She played it off, but remembered how against it he'd been the first time she brought it up—

"That's fine," he said, a little closer. "And I'm not going anywhere until I know if Ashley's all right."

She wasn't surprised by his answer, feeling the same way herself, wet dress or not. Then she glanced at him. "Drink?"

"Why not?" he muttered, taking a seat at the piano.

Heading into the kitchen, Remi opened up one of the cabinets, taking a moment to look at the marks on her dress again. She hadn't been sure when she answered Desmond, but none of them were serious. Neither of them had been injured, and that was lucky. Except she didn't believe in luck.

Thomas had said it was remotely detonated. That meant someone watched them head to the car and set it off before they were inside. Was that intentional? That would leave them scared. Send them running. Panicking. Except she hadn't done that. They were safe here. A warning, then? Had the attacker not seen them? Was it poor timing? Nonetheless, remotes didn't work all that far away. The attacker had to have been at the party.

Remi grabbed two crystal tumblers and the scotch Desmond drank the other morning. Pouring a generous measure into each, she returned to the living room. She heard Desmond start playing something on the piano. It wasn't something she'd heard before, but it was slow and melancholy. To fit with the mood, she supposed. She grabbed a coaster off the coffee table and put his drink on the piano.

"Thank you," he said, never stopping in his playing.

"Sure." She stood off to the side, watching his

hands move across the keys far easier than hers had. He didn't seem to be thinking about it as he played. She sipped the scotch, holding it in her mouth to make it burn, then turning back to the window.

She stared out at the glass, not seeing anything but her reflection. She stared back at herself: wet, bedraggled hair and a dragging white dress streaked with rain and ash. She was a disaster. A goddamn embarrassment. She should've seen the bomb coming. She should have been more observant. She shouldn't have forgotten her goal, not even for a second.

"I'm sorry." She said it more to herself, but he heard her.

The piano paused, and she heard the ice clink against the glass. "What for?"

"I should've seen it coming. I should've been more careful, and we got fucking lucky, because—"

"Remi." He stood and walked toward her, his reflection growing in the glass as he approached, tumbler in hand. She didn't turn, meeting his eyes in the reflection as he stopped behind her.

"It's like you said, isn't it?" His words brushed her bare shoulder. "This isn't your fault. It's theirs. They're doing this, and we can't know what's going to happen, because none of this makes sense. They attacked us in your home. The place you're supposed to feel safe. There were cops and security, and no one saw this coming. You have nothing to be sorry for."

She looked away from his reflection, not convinced, but feeling less guilty. He was right. She couldn't control everything. She'd done everything by the book. She'd followed the rules and her judgment, and they were both still alive. That meant she must be doing something right.

Letting out a long breath, she took a sip of her drink. She glanced at her phone again, anxious to hear from Thomas. Without looking up, she turned, finding Desmond close behind her.

His eyes flickered up to hers. The worry that had been in them earlier eased somewhat. He didn't step back, tucking a piece of her damp hair behind her ear.

Remi shivered but didn't step away. She hated to admit it, but she wished they were back at that dance. Desmond's arm around her, holding her against him. She wanted that again, but closer and a bit more private. Instead of trying to drive him home, she wished they'd snuck off to her room and...

Desmond didn't drop his hand, his thumb running over her cheek. It was so light it felt like maybe it was happening. But it was, and she didn't want it to stop.

She took a half step nearer, so close she could feel the heat from Desmond's skin, smell the scotch on his breath. A tiny, tiny voice, which sounded an awful lot like Ashley, told her this was a bad idea, but she silenced it. She was beyond caring, beyond considering, and jumping into this with both feet and no life jacket. She heard Desmond's breath hitch as she tilted her face up, and his lips curled up as he leaned down—

Remi's phone rang.

She and Desmond both jumped, moving away from one another.

"Shit." She glanced at the display, seeing Thomas's name. Her annoyance at the interruption vanished and she answered immediately.

"Is everyone okay?" she asked, putting the phone on speaker.

Thomas sounded tired but calm. "Miss Graves and Mr. O'Brien are fine." Desmond breathed out a sigh of relief, putting his glass on the counter and smiling a little easier. "Everyone is okay. Samara took Rick and Ashley to the safehouse on 16th Street, so we couldn't track their phones. Everyone is okay. One of the drivers is in the hospital, but he's expected to make a full recovery."

"Thank you." Relief poured into her stomach. She took the phone off speaker and raised it to her ear. "Seriously, Thomas. Thanks."

"I'll have security on the apartment and work by Monday, but not until then."

"That's fine. I've got my bag. I'll stay." Her eyes tracked Desmond in the kitchen, washing out his glass.

"If you don't feel up to it, Cam or I may be able—"

She interrupted him. "I've got this."

"Be careful," Thomas said.

"Always am."

"Liar."

She said goodbye and hung up, looking at Desmond. "Everyone's okay."

"Yeah." He smiled. "That's great."

They stared at one another for a moment, neither of them making a move. Thomas's call, though necessary and appreciated, also had kind of put a hold on the...moment.

Remi smiled, then stepped back from the kitchen. "We should get cleaned up. Get some rest."

"Right." He cleared his throat, lifted her bag from the from the floor hall and walked her to the spare room. She'd been in it every night since she started working, but she appreciated the gesture.

The queen bed looked inviting when she stepped in, the gray comforter soft and thick. The lights were off, but enough light came from the hallway to see by.

"Towels are in the guest bathroom closet." He placed her bag on the floor. "If you need anything—"

"I know where you are." Remi smiled.

He chuckled, rubbing the back of his neck. "Of course. Goodnight."

"'Night, Des."

Stepping to the door, he made to close it, but hesitated. That hesitation was almost her undoing, but he shook his head and closed the door with a click.

Remi let out a breath, the sound shaking in the dark.

****

Desmond shut his bedroom door a little harder than necessary. Leaning against it, he loosened his tie with one hand, undoing the top button.

They'd been so close…

The rain was a constant hush around him, pattering against his window. He shed his jacket, praying his dry cleaner could rescue it. Putting his cufflinks in their usual tray, he caught his reflection.

Whatever these…feelings with Remi were, they were overtaking every thought he had. He should've been terrified about Rick and Ashley, and he had been, but not enough to keep him from touching her. He closed his eyes, the memory of Remi up against him at the dance lighting up his skin. What he wouldn't give for another chance.

Well, what was stopping him now?

His doubts appeared and vanished in a matter of seconds.

He was a job—no, they were closer, and she'd said as much.

She didn't feel the same way—he saw the way she leaned up to him now.

They shouldn't get distracted—they were safe and secure tonight.

It was a risk—sure, but what worthwhile things weren't?

He'd never felt this way about anyone before, and he was tired of everything else getting in the way. Tonight, they were alone, and if he didn't take a chance, he was going to regret it forever.

Making up his mind, he stalked to the door, throwing it open—

To see Remi on the other side, her hand raised to knock. Her gaze darted over him, taking in all the tiny details that only she noticed, before meeting his. He swallowed. Hard.

Even soaked and ash-streaked, she had to be the most beautiful woman in the world.

Her hair was starting to come down, clumped together in wet strands. The white dress clung to her, dirtied from the explosion. She'd thrown off the heels, leaving her almost head and shoulders shorter than him. It struck him how tiny she was. All that raw power compressed into such a small, striking, sarcastic, foul-mouthed package.

His life had been so simple before her. He had his work. His sister. Rick. Now, he had…friends. A social life. Plans. His life now was so much louder, more dangerous, messier, more complicated—

Better.

Desmond stared down at her for a long moment,

his hands gripping the handle and the frame. He was sure of what he wanted but uncertain on how to get there.

Then Remi, brave and brilliant Remi, said, "I want this. Do you?"

"Yes."

"Thank fucking God," she muttered, grabbing his tie and pulling him toward her.

She didn't need to pull; he was halfway toward her already. One arm wrapped around her waist, her bare skin cool from the wet and the rain, but still lighting him on fire. He had the presence of mind to pull her into the room and shut the door behind her before he was completely lost.

Remi's shoulders knocked back into the door as Desmond pressed against her. She laughed breathlessly, the sound disappearing between his lips. The taste of scotch and copper was harsh and addictive on his tongue, even as hands cupped his face. And that was everything with Remi—an external rush that belied her good heart.

He wove his free hand into her hair, holding her against him, not that her grip on his tie was relenting at all. He kissed her with everything he'd been holding back. Alternating teeth scraping, rough kisses, he soothed them with softer, slower ones. When he broke away for breath, Remi panted with him, her hands running over his face and shoulders. Her lips were red and swollen and twisted into that familiar smirk.

"I knew you'd be amazing," she murmured.

He laughed, that invincible feeling that came with the courtroom coming in full force as he looked at her. "Oh, Archer." He pressed another kiss against her smiling mouth. "You haven't seen anything yet."

Pulling her hands away from his tie, Desmond dropped to his knees in front of her.

Remi leaned her head back against the door with a faint thud. "Oh, God."

He ran his hands up along her ankles, beneath the white dress. It fell away on one side, the invisible slit when the skirt was dry revealed in the sodden lines. Desmond continued to push up, his mouth following the path his hands took. Every new inch revealed toned, golden skin, marked and crossed with scars. Midway along her thigh, Desmond encountered fabric. He sat back on his heels, glancing at the thigh holster holding three knives.

"Your formal holster?" He slid his fingers along the back to unbuckle it.

She laughed. "Only the best for you."

He liked the sound of that, dropping the holster to the side before resuming his journey. Remi shivered beneath him, her hands running over the top of his head.

"How's your balance?" he asked against her skin.

"What—oh!"

Desmond slid one hand underneath the back of her knee, lifting it over his shoulder. He grabbed her other hip with his free hand, keeping her steady.

"I've got you," he promised. Moving aside the white—God, she looked good in white—scrap of fabric keeping her from view, he dived in.

This was one of his favorite things to do. Not only because he enjoyed it, but because it was difficult to do well, and he'd always excelled at the difficult. He thrived on accomplishing what people said was impossible. Being both good and willing to do this made it impossible for most people. It made him unforgettable.

Right now, it was his favorite thing because he got a rush from hearing the sounds she made. From feeling the way her hands scrabbled for a grip and finding nothing to keep her from falling. From tasting the honey of her desire for him and from seeing gold skin shivering beneath his lips and hands. This powerful, controlled woman lost her composure when it came to him. And when she cried out, it was his name that fell from her lips.

He could listen to that sound forever.

Desmond waited, giving her a moment until the tremors slowed somewhat. He dropped her leg off of his shoulder as he rose. She opened her eyes when he grasped her waist, and he felt another thrill of accomplishment as he saw dazed blue.

He chuckled and she refocused, glaring at him without any real feeling. "You look proud."

"Oh, I am."

She kissed him fiercely, bringing him back to the brink he'd been hanging over in mere seconds. She turned them around, his back against the door now and her pressing against him. One hand tangled in her hair, those golden strands wrapped around his fingers. He kissed every part of her he could reach, her lips, her face, her neck, her shoulders. She grabbed his hands from where they'd settled on her waist and drew them up. Over her hips and up her sides, before she deposited them on the thin straps on top of her shoulders.

For all his bravado, he felt his hands tremor as he nudged the straps down over her shoulders. He followed them down over her wrists, feeling the fabric tumble down to the floor. His fingers smoothed back up to her shoulders before she stepped back enough for him to see her.

He swallowed, his eyes catching everything. Every inch, every scar, every blemish he acknowledged because each mark made her who she was. This fierce, hilarious, kind-hearted, protective woman. He wouldn't trade her for the world. "Perfect."

"Bullshit." She wasn't shy, but not oblivious to what she saw as her imperfections.

"Perfect," he repeated, his arms sliding around her. If she didn't believe him, he'd be happy to tell her every day for the rest of his life, if she'd let him.

That thought bounced in his head, making him draw back for a moment. But Remi's lips were far more important, so he pushed the thought aside for later.

But in his heart, he knew it was too late.

****

Remi shivered, a combination of cold, desire, and aftershocks still rolling through her. Her bare skin was against Desmond's wet suit, and she pulled away from him, stepping back toward his bed.

"Too many clothes." She grabbed his tie, undoing the knot and sliding the fabric from beneath the collar. Desmond followed her, his eyes dark as he started undoing the buttons on his shirt.

Perfect, he'd said.

Lovers had called her beautiful before, but she'd always written it off as pillow talk. Because even if there were qualities about her that made her memorable, she wasn't beautiful. She was too scarred and too messed up and too angry to be beautiful.

But he'd called her perfect. Perfect, or perfect for him? Because she very much preferred one of those options over the other.

He pulled his shirt away and threw it to the side, his arms back around her before it hit the floor. Skin pressed against skin, and she was no longer cold. Everything was hot, her skin, his breath, his hands. Everything felt like fire licking against her skin, and if it was going to consume her, she'd die happy. Her arms went around his neck, the groan that escaped his lips muffled by her mouth. She preened—he'd driven her crazy in mere minutes; it was only fair she could do the same.

With his arm around her back, he lowered her to the bed, the plush comforter cool, but not cold. Desmond followed her, his weight pressing her into the bed in the best kind of way. Without thinking about it, she rolled her hips beneath him. He broke away, a haggard breath escaping.

"Remi—" Whatever he was going to say faded away with a groan as she did it again.

She grinned, glad that she could break through all the cold lawyer bullshit to the real Desmond Graves. The one she felt like she'd known for years as opposed to weeks. The one currently using his teeth in a very interesting manner on her neck.

Shimmying her hands between them, she popped the button on his slacks and undid the zipper. Her fingers brushed against the cut of his hip and made him buck against her.

Hooking her foot around his knee, she flipped them. She shoved his slacks down around his knees and onto the floor before she settled against his hips, only his briefs separating them.

She shifted, watching Desmond's eyes slam shut and his jaw clench as she rubbed along him. His hands grabbed her waist, his fingers pressing into her so hard he might leave bruises. She did it again and he almost growled beneath her, his eyes opening and completely black. She leaned down and kissed him, her hips still rolling against him.

"Remi." He interspersed the syllables with burning kisses. "Please."

Damn, he could ask for anything in that tone of voice and she'd give it to him.

Sliding down his body, she grabbed his briefs and pulled them down. Settling between his hips, she didn't give him any time to prepare before taking him into her mouth.

"Jesus—" He choked back what he'd been about to say, his hands fisting on the bedspread. Remi hollowed out her cheeks and Desmond's hand flew to the back of her head, her name coming out in strangled tones. It was damn empowering, to be honest.

After only a few more seconds, Desmond stopped her. "Remi, wait, I want—"

She pulled away, looking up at him. "Want what?"

He sat up, and she rose next to him. His hand cupped her face, his eyes dark but not clouded. "You."

Desmond kissed her, quite unlike the earlier ones. It burned with heat and urgency, yes. But something much slower and deeper rolled between them like a shockwave. Straddling his hips again without breaking the kiss, she didn't let him lie back. His hands roamed over her back, one tangling in her hair as he held her close. The taste of his lips made her restless, grinding against him. Her arms were around his neck, her hand scraping over his hair and jaw.

Desmond didn't move back, not much, only enough to mumble, "Condom—"

"IUD," she said. "And clean. You?"

"Of course."

"Thank God." She kissed him again as she raised herself just enough and slid back down on him. She let out a stuttering breath as he filled her.

Desmond's hands were like vises around her, holding her against him as if they could become one. She didn't normally buy into that romantic bullshit, but God, she wanted it to be true right now.

She rose, sliding back down along him inch by inch. Desmond groaned, kissing her until she was completely breathless. For all their intense start, she smiled to find that the slow, intimate pace was what they needed.

Her previous one-night stands were rushed and extreme, chased with dissatisfaction and scotch. Nothing about this felt rushed, and though intense, she'd never call it extreme. There wasn't going to be any dissatisfaction, and the only scotch she'd drink afterward would be with him.

She rose again, kissing every bit of Desmond she could reach, his face, his jaw, his cheeks. She kept her eyes open, not wanting to miss a moment of this. Not the way his jaw clenched each time she slid down as if she didn't love every indecent sound that slipped out of him. Not the way his eyes remained laser-focused on her face like he was trying to memorize it. Not the way his lips formed words that he didn't speak, and that she pretended not to understand, not yet.

This wasn't a one-night stand, but that's all she was willing to admit now.

His hands dug into her skin, clenching and unclenching, and she knew he was close. Which made it all the more startling when he tilted them over, pushing her back into the bed and leaning over her.

"Not without you," he growled. One of those hands, those damn clever fingers, found its way between them. He twisted and worked her until she trembled beneath him, never losing the rhythm.

Her breath coming short, she squeezed her eyes shut. "Fuck."

"Remi, look at me. Look at me."

She forced her eyes open, Desmond leaned over her, a breath away. His lips brushed hers and the angle was right and his fingers—

"Des!" She cried out as lights exploded behind her eyes. She threw her head back, riding out the aftershocks. She felt him kiss her throat, his hand shifting to her hip to pull her harder against him.

She did her best to catch her breath, rolling against him when he moved forward. She grinned when he met her eyes. "Come on, hotshot."

He leaned down to kiss her hard, his teeth scraping her lip. Remi ran her hands over his back, pulling him against her until she couldn't tell their heartbeats apart. A breath, then his grip tightened. The most obscene, "Remi," she'd ever heard in her life slipped from his lips to hers. She would never forget the way it tasted.

Remi lay there, wrapped up in Desmond, his breath hot against her neck. Between one heartbeat and the next, her head caught up with what her heart had known for weeks. As he lifted himself, he gave her a soft smile, looking so vulnerable. She kissed him, and it felt much more important than anything they just did.

Desmond Graves was a prim, arrogant, brilliant, stubborn, loyal, pain in the ass.

And she was in love with him.

****

Several hours later, the moonlight had crawled away to the edge of the windows. Shadows escaped from the piles of discarded clothing, muffling the glitter of a knife. It softened the breaths from Remi as she slept on the large, empty bed, the sheet pulled up to her waist. Her hand reached out, encountering nothing but the shadows.

In the living room, the shadows were a little darker, heavier. They clung to the feet of the piano, dragged the curtains down, pooling beneath the folds. In the kitchen, the dark scotch in a glass at Desmond's elbow seemed almost black. His head rested in his hands as he sat at the kitchen table, his papers, phone, and briefcase spread out before him. Lifting his head, he looked out the window, staring out into nothing. He didn't move, didn't breathe, and then—

"What have I done?"

But only shadows heard him.

Chapter Ten

Despite last night's activities, Remi's internal clock remained reliable as ever. As she opened her eyes, then stretched, aches and pains from overused muscles helped in the waking process. Desmond was nowhere in sight, but she didn't worry too much about it. She smelled coffee coming from the kitchen. Getting to her feet, she grabbed his striped shirt from the day before and pulled it on. It hit her thigh, the cuffs dangling over her hands. She buttoned it up, but if they were going to be on house arrest until everything calmed down, she could think of several ways to pass the time. None included this shirt.

Last night had been amazing. Everything she'd imagined, then a hundred percent more. She was lucky to find a guy like Desmond. Someone who respected her and treated her as an equal and who wasn't frightened off by her past or her attitude. Someone who understood what it was like to feel like you weren't worth anything and be working on fixing that. Someone who cared about her, all the good and bad things included.

In bare feet, she wandered into the other room, and found him at the window. He was dressed, though in his more casual jeans and sweater. She must have slept well not to hear him moving around. He was staring out the window, a mug of coffee in his hand.

Another of her stray thoughts insinuated itself in her head, thinking it would be nice to wake up to him every day. She smiled, putting it aside, though not as far as she usually did. The sunlight warmed the quiet room, turning everything gold.

Giving in to the urge, she approached and wrapped her arms around him, resting her cheek against his back. "Morning." It was as soft as she thought it would be. "Sleep well?"

He didn't answer. And stepped out of her hug.

Remi tilted her head at him. "What's going on?"

He still said nothing, so Remi grabbed his arm to turn him around. "Des, come on, what's—"

He turned, no trace of a smile on his face. No trace of anything. Not even a memory of the emotions that had played across his expression last night.

Her stomach began to churn. "Hey. Is everything okay?"

"No." The word was clipped, almost cold.

"What happened?" Her anger rose in reaction to his. Whatever it was, she'd take care of it, and he'd be okay, but she had to know—

Desmond stared past her. "I don't feel safe."

The words were simple. Nothing over a syllable, but they made no sense in her head. She stared at him, unable to say anything other than a strangled, "What?"

"I said, I don't feel safe. I'd like someone else assigned to my case." He walked past her to the kitchen where his briefcase and work papers sat organized on the table.

"Since when?"

Remi followed him, unable to keep away. Her bare feet hit the tile of his kitchen floor, the cold stealing up her legs. She regretted dressing in only his shirt. She felt like an idiot, some love-struck moron mooning over a man who didn't—

"Last night."

"Last night." She stopped in her tracks, feeling too exposed in the harsh sunlight. "Was it before or after?"

He sighed, turning to face her. "It's complicated, and—"

"Don't take that condescending tone with me," she barked. "Before or after?"

"When the explosion—"

"So before," she said, falling silent for a moment. "I...I asked you if you wanted—wanted this. And you said yes."

He still didn't look at her. "I'm sorry."

"Don't apologize." Her hands began to shake. This wasn't some missed birthday or forgotten date. This was so much worse, and he was apologizing like it meant nothing.

"But I am." His voice had become her favorite sound, but now she wanted him to stop talking. "I'm very sorry that this didn't work out, but I don't feel safe anymore."

"You felt safe enough to fuck me."

He flinched. "I got caught up in the moment, but it was a..."

"A mistake." Remi finished it for him.

Desmond didn't disagree. He didn't say anything.

Remi's breath wasn't coming. Her heart had relocated into her throat, choking her, but she'd be damned if she let him see how much it hurt. She turned away, trying to get her temper under control. Her hands shook, and her cheeks burned, and she wanted to throw up, to scream, to walk out and never look at him again. She wanted to hate him, she did, but she couldn't.

Her damn traitorous heart.

She paused, turning to face him, though he seemed unwilling to meet her eyes. "Did something happen?" There had to be some explanation for his behavior, that it wasn't because he didn't care. "Was there another letter or something? Because I can take these assholes, you don't need to protect me. And I—"

"There's no letter." He gestured at the table. "You can look."

And there went her last hope.

"Right," she said. "Of course." She was an idiot to think they could have worked out on a personal level. He was Desmond Graves, lawyer and hero. She was an employable murderer for hire—and an idiot for thinking he could love her.

"I just…" He hesitated, but his voice was calm. Certain. "I can't help the way I feel. Or don't."

Like how he didn't feel safe. Like how he didn't feel what she did.

"We can," she started, having to clear her throat, "we can go back to the way things were, I can still help—"

"I appreciate it. But I'd prefer someone else." Such a polite tone. The same condescending tone he'd used with the defense in Landon's case. The same tone he used with Landon. The tone he used with everyone he thought was beneath him.

All the anger and fury went out of her. She wasn't a trained soldier. She wasn't a bodyguard. She was a heartbroken fool, and she had to get out of here. She had to leave because she couldn't handle him looking at her like this, not for one more second. Not after the way he looked at her last night.

"Fine." Her mouth felt numb. Clumsy. "I'll get someone else."

She turned and walked to the spare room, made a phone call to Exceptional Security, and dressed in record time. When she was ready, she sat on the edge of the bed, too much of a coward to face him.

She stared at the wall, trying to figure out where it'd gone wrong, but she couldn't focus. With every shift, she felt the aches of last night. Every hard swallow of her throat brought memories of his lips. Her fisted hands on her lap reminded her of how hard he'd held her, bruising her skin.

Her phone buzzed. Camille was downstairs.

She grabbed her bag, hauling it over her shoulder as she stepped out into the hallway. Desmond was at his desk, typing something into his computer. She stopped in front of him, unsure of what to say. He never even looked up. She decided to say nothing and walked past.

When she got to the door, he called after her. "Goodbye, Archer."

She didn't respond, shutting the door behind her and leaving Desmond behind.

****

Remi rolled into Exceptional Security late Sunday morning. The tight jeans and skimpy top she'd worn out to the club still reeked of sweat and alcohol. Her head pounded but continued on, removing the sunglasses as she limped down the hall.

Gemma looked up at her as she entered, her lips pressing together.

"I don't want to hear a word." Remi tossed the

glasses onto the desk, her throat burning. She blinked against the bright lights, rubbing her temple.

Gemma nodded. "Thomas is out of the office for the day."

Remi heard the hidden message—*clean your shit up or else.*

Heading upstairs, she grabbed some clothes out of her room. She didn't encounter anyone as she wandered toward the bathroom. It should be empty. Samara had passed Remi in the hallway, not saying anything, and Camille—

Camille had Remi's job to do.

Remi stripped in the bathroom, keeping her eyes away from the mirror. Soon the steam from the scalding water had fogged it up. She stepped in, watching her skin immediately flush red, then stuck her head under the spray.

She tried going out to a club, drinking, and dancing with strangers. She'd hoped that their hands and kisses might erase whatever memories she hadn't numbed with alcohol. But whenever someone put their hand on her waist, she couldn't help but compare it. No one's hands were wide enough, or warm enough, or moved the right way, or felt like enough—

So she drank more and kept trying. A woman who'd bought her drinks tried to kiss her, and Remi thought it was okay. Until the last moment, when she turned away, letting the girl catch her cheek instead. No matter how much she drank, she wouldn't be able to forget the way he felt. A stupid, weak little part of her didn't want to.

She closed her eyes and regretted it immediately. The hot water came closer to his touch than anything else. She could see bright blue eyes, blown out and dark, leaning over her and promising—

Remi turned the tap, enduring the burst of cold water to drive away any residual memories.

Promising nothing.

She got out and dried off. Wiping her face, she shoved the palms of her hands into her eyes until she saw spots. She tried to wipe away everything because this was wrecking her.

In sweatpants and a tank top, she went back to her room. As she opened the door, she paused, still squeezing water out of her hair.

Samara, Alec, and Gemma were there.

She hung her towel on her door as she closed it behind her. "What's going on?"

"We want you to know that we're here for you. And we want to help you in any way that—"

"Shut up, Alec," Samara cut in. "Here." She handed Remi a big cup of coffee.

Remi took it, sitting on the chair by her desk, sipping the drink. When it was clear she wasn't going to speak, Gemma sighed and leaned forward. "What happened with you and Mr. Graves?"

Remi scoffed. "Nothing, I—"

"Remi," Samara interrupted. "You two were inseparable, and then he bails? Since when? What the hell happened?"

"He said he didn't feel safe and would prefer someone else." She got that out without her voice trembling.

"So what happened?" Alec asked.

Remi got to her feet, leaving the cup on her desk. "Nothing happened, we—"

"Bullshit." Samara sat back, frowning.

"Remi—"

"I fucked up, okay?"

Alec and Samara drew back, but Gemma didn't seem surprised.

Now with the dam broken, Remi couldn't stop. "I messed up. I got distracted and emotionally compromised, and he saw it, so now we're done." She leaned against the wall, crossing her arms to keep her chest from splitting open.

"You slept with him," Gemma said, after a moment of quiet.

Remi's head jerked up, staring her in the eye. "Yeah. Yes. Stupid."

"I don't think so," Alec said, having recovered from her outburst.

"Oh yeah? Why's that?"

"Well, you love him."

Remi swallowed, unable to find the breath to disagree or to argue. She couldn't think of anything to say to keep her dignity.

"And Desmond?" Gemma asked, shifting on the bed to make room.

"Well, I'm not there any longer, so his feelings are pretty clear." She took Gemma's unspoken offer and sat down, Alec taking the chair so he could face them.

"Eh, I don't think so," Samara said. "He couldn't keep his eyes off you at the party, he's into you." When everyone looked at her, she glared. "What? I pay attention."

"Doesn't matter about the party. He asked for someone else," Remi said. "He said he didn't feel safe. I'm not going to pressure him."

"But you love him." Alec leaned forward.

"So?" Remi said. "It's probably what made him...he figured I was too distracted."

"You caring is a distraction?" Gemma asked. "Don't you think it makes you more attentive and willing to go the extra mile?"

Remi shrugged. "It doesn't matter. It matters what he wants, and that's not me."

Alec shook his head. "You're wrong. You two are made for each other."

"Thanks. But that doesn't mean much right now."

They sat in silence. Remi rubbed her temples in an attempt to erase the ache behind her eyes.

"What do you need?" Samara asked.

Remi dropped her hands. "I need...for him to be okay."

"Then we keep working on the case," Alec said. "We figure out, once and for all, what's going on. And when it's done, you can be together."

That was optimistic, but she appreciated the gesture.

"This isn't over." Samara touched her arm. "I can always beat the stupid out of him."

Remi laughed. It was a short, hard sound, but still a laugh. "Thanks. Really. Now, go away before Alec starts braiding our hair."

"Let's go, Boy Scout." Samara grabbed Alec's elbow and towed him toward the door.

"Actually, it was Eagle Scouts. I earned a merit badge in—"

Gemma stood, smoothing her skirt and glancing at Remi. "What else can I do for you, Miss Archer?"

Remi resisted the urge to hug her; shit, she'd gotten

so soft in the past two weeks. "I'd like to keep busy."

"I can arrange that. Thomas has some upcoming consultations, and I'm sure he'd appreciate your insight," Gemma said. She strode toward the door, grasping the handle and stepping out. Midway through the threshold, she paused. "For what it's worth, I agree with Mr. Singh. You two are well suited for each other. This will work out."

"Thanks, Gemma."

The door closed behind her. Remi didn't move for a couple of minutes, trying to come to terms with everything they'd said. Then she stood, downed the coffee, and pulled out Desmond's file.

Time to get to work.

****

Monday morning, Desmond woke with his alarm. He took a shower, got dressed. He made his coffee. His phone buzzed and displayed a text.

—Good morning. I'm downstairs.—

Desmond put on his jacket and grabbed his briefcase before sliding his phone into his pocket. Taking the stairs, he looked up, a flash of blonde hair near the door making him stumble. But the woman walked past the door and revealed Camille Juma. Desmond stepped out, nodding at her. "Morning."

"Good morning, Mr. Graves. How did you sleep?"

"Fine."

She took his not-so-subtle hint for no talking and spent the walk to his office in silence. He kept his eyes up and moving, avoiding car doors as they opened, stepping around people to keep them out of arm's reach. Camille was attentive, with no sign of a smile on her face as she did the same.

She hadn't been as talkative as when he'd seen her the night of the party. A tension he knew he was responsible for prevented conversation. He couldn't blame her. He knew exactly who was to blame.

They got to the courts building; Camille walked him to the door. "I'll see you at lunch."

"I'll be working through lunch," he said.

"All right. Call if you need anything. I'll be here."

"Thanks."

Desmond stepped through the lobby and entered the staff elevator. He was early enough that the walk to his office was solitary, which was exactly the way he wanted it. Dropping his briefcase on his desk, he shut the door, wanting some quiet as he worked through the Jesse Randall file. At least the arson case would keep his mind occupied. Pulling out the files, he took his seat behind his desk and placed the documents in order. He began skimming the arrest report.

Witnesses saw Randall fleeing the scene of the crime, the gold—

Gold hair splayed across his comforter as he'd leaned over Remi. Her impish grin was unapologetic as she rolled against him. He kissed it off her lips, pressing against her, and he needed her so badly it hurt—

Desmond cleared his throat, refocusing on the documents.

Firefighters confirmed that the fire began in the vault, before spreading to the rest of the bank. Descriptions of the fire's color and the intense heat—

"Come on, hotshot," she'd said beneath him. Absurdly innocent words for her, but the tone made it the hottest thing he'd heard in his life. Her cheeks were still flushed, her breath still panting between her lips.

Desmond decided he could live on this feeling, hovering over the edge, as long as she was there to catch him—

He stood, dropping the papers and pacing in front of his window, trying to catch his breath. Was this his punishment? Being forced to relive this memory for eternity? Because what exquisite torture it would be. Grabbing the file, he remained standing.

Footprints leading from the scene of the explosion—

—behind his eyes as her mouth wrapped around him. He choked back the swears that filled his throat, his hand tangling in her hair. He wasn't anticipating this, despite his earlier actions. Her tongue ran up him, and he started to see stars. He needed to stop because he wanted her this first time, only her—

He rubbed his eyes, cursing himself and trying again.

...might have been a perfect crime—

"Perfect," he'd murmured. Battered and bruised, she was the most powerful, beautiful woman he'd ever seen. Her pale skin, gold hair, her bright eyes. How did she not see how amazing she was?

He grabbed his coffee off the table, trying to drown out the dry taste in his mouth. Trying to drown the memories of how she tasted. She tainted every piece of food he'd forced into his leaden stomach.

—breaking in while the residents were asleep.

He'd snuck out of bed, Remi's hand slipping out of his as he left. As he grabbed a pair of sweatpants, his eyes drifted back to her where the sheets draped over her shoulders and her lips parted in sleep. He'd smiled, unable to resist bending down and pressing his lips to her cheek, not enough to wake her. Before he left, he took one last look, memorizing the sight of her in his bed. Hopefully, he would see this for many days to come. But right now, he had work to catch up on. So he left their bed like a thief in the night and—

He clenched his fist, leaning against his window. Turning his eyes to his work, he tried to focus one last time. He was a professional.

Witnesses claimed Randall wanted—

"I want this. Do you?"

He threw the file onto his desk, knocking the metal pencil holder onto the ground with a clatter. As pens rolled across the ground, he heard a knock at the door. "What?" he barked.

Nelson, a younger intern, poked his head in. "Sorry to bother you, Mr. Graves…" He trailed off, looking at the mess on the floor.

"What was it?" Desmond tried to moderate his tone, but from the way Nelson swallowed, it hadn't worked.

"You're needed in the conference room."

"Thank you. I'll be there."

Nelson nodded, shutting the door behind him.

Desmond took a deep breath, exhaling through his nose. He was a fool. A selfish and arrogant fool to think he could have anything good when people like Delaney were after him. He glanced at his phone, swallowing past the lump in his throat. He brought this on himself. He would pay, whatever price demanded. Even if it drove him mad.

The phone he was glaring at started ringing, and he saw his sister's name on the display. "Ash," he said, slouching into his chair. "Everything okay?"

"Yeah," she said, sounding a little subdued. "Um, Samara let something slip, so I wanted to check on you. She said you and Remi—"

There was only one thing Samara could have let slip about Remi. "I'm fine," he interrupted.

"Hey, if you wanna get together for a drink tonight…"

"Thanks. But I…I've got a lot of work to do."

"Oh, okay." She was quiet for a long moment. "You sure?"

"Thanks. I need to focus on work. Maybe some other time."

"Okay. It's gonna be okay."

"Yeah." That was a lie.

Chapter Eleven

"Hey, Remi, Thomas wants—Holy shit."

Remi turned as Samara opened her door. The dark-skinned woman stopped in the frame as she stared into the room. Throughout the small space, lines and notes connected papers, photos, and logs of prison incarcerations and visits. This had been her life the past several days, and it took Remi a long moment to realize it was only Thursday.

Samara leaned against the door. "Well, if I didn't know you so well, I'd think you were Graves's stalker."

"Ha." Remi grabbed her jacket and swung it on. "What does Thomas want?"

"His consult is here. Thought you'd want to sit in on it."

Wanted and needed were two different things, and Remi needed to stay busy. "Yeah. Thanks."

As they walked toward the stairs, Samara glanced over to her. "Anything new?"

"Not yet," Remi admitted. "Gemma and I have been working through the payments that were being split with Landon. Alec is looking for DNA from the letters Graves got earlier, but the only winner so far is mine and Graves's. Thomas and Farid have been tracking Delaney every second. But the one case we thought connected it all is over, and Desmond still received a letter. So what the hell do they want?"

"We're gonna figure this out," Samara murmured.

"I know." She rubbed her eyes. "How's Ashley?"

Samara shrugged. "Stubborn. But she checks in and wears her tracker."

"Good."

"Rick's been a bit of a shit to train, but he should do well."

"I'm glad Thomas followed through with him." She glanced at her phone, seeing it was five past the hour. "Okay. Keep me updated. See you later."

"Have fun," Samara called after her.

Remi jogged down to the conference room, coming up right behind Thomas and two people in suits. One was darker and had a familiar smile. The other just stared at her with heavy brown eyes. Remi forced a smile.

Thomas gestured to her. "Gentlemen, meet Miss Remi Archer. Miss Archer, this is Mr. Nassar, Farid's father. And Director Sanchez. They work for an undisclosed government agency and were looking for a consult."

Remi nodded as she shook their hands. "Nice to meet you."

After they filed into the room, they each took seats around a heavy table. The tinted windows lent an ominous light to the room. For that reason alone, she'd always preferred the upstairs conference room to this one. She took a seat next to Thomas as Mr. Nassar pulled papers from a briefcase.

"Care to fill us in on what's been happening so far?" Thomas said, taking out his notebook.

Director Sanchez leaned forward, his thick fingers pushing a file toward them. "We have a stalking situation, and it's not like anything we've seen."

"You haven't seen anything, yet."

—As wet, hot heat enveloped her, Remi couldn't help the sounds that escaped from between her lips. She made the mistake of looking down as Desmond looked up, his eyes bright and dark, and his mouth—

She cleared her throat, flipping through the pages without seeing them. "The target?"

"An American government official," Mr. Nassar said, speaking with the authority and using vague terms most unnamed agencies preferred. "We think he's being leaned on to repeal a recent vote. There have been anonymous payments to his bank account under the guise of campaign donations, but he doesn't accept any of them. We're concerned that if he doesn't give in to their kinder methods, they're going to escalate. We don't feel—"

"I can't help the way I feel. Or don't."

The words were like lead in her stomach, weighing her down, dragging her under the regret she wished she felt. She wished she could hate him because that would be so much easier—

She grabbed the bottled water in front of her, took a long sip.

"We're looking for advice for what to watch out for, how to predict their movements and make sure we're not falling—"

Falling in love with him hadn't been a choice. She would've refused. Not because he wasn't worth it, because she knew he was. Not even because she thought she wasn't worth it.

Remi swayed in his arms, Desmond wrapped around her. He held her close, his breath brushing against her cheek.

She would've refused because this was the kind of love that could make or break a person. And she'd been broken too many times. She wasn't certain she could survive another one.

"…advice, Miss Archer?" Thomas was saying.

Remi looked up at him. "Sorry, what?"

"Advice for our guests?" Thomas frowned at her, his demand to get her act together and pay attention clear. "What to watch out for."

"In, um…in my experience." Remi cleared her throat. "With the amount of money they've shown, you're dealing with a group or a well-connected individual. If the more passive actions don't work, they'll escalate. Look for minor inconveniences: his car stops working, papers go missing, threats, veiled or otherwise. If you keep the mark paranoid, it makes them easier to manipulate."

Sanchez's eyes were fixed on her. "And if they do escalate? What might they do?"

She looked over at him, considering the question. "If it were me, I'd alienate the mark. Keep them from help. I'd make sure they felt isolated. Make them feel like it was them against me. Turn them against their friends or vice versa. Make them vulnerable or desperate. I might even go after people they care about, like a wife or daughter…" She trailed off, staring past Thomas.

"Remi?"

"I'm sorry, excuse me for a minute." She stood, ignoring his glare and the confused looks on the clients' faces. Her chair spun behind her as she ran toward the door. It slammed shut in her wake and she got to the front lobby in record time.

Gemma was at the desk and jumped when Remi shouted her name. "Yes, Miss Archer?"

"Do you have access to Graves's phone?"

"I can, yes, but—"

"Pull it up. Show me any messages from Friday and Saturday."

Gemma stared at her for a moment, then turned her chair. She pulled up a program that displayed Desmond's home screen, remotely accessed.

"Anything?" Remi asked, leaning forward.

Gemma scrolled through the texts, but Remi only saw the ones from her and a couple from Ashley. "Nothing out of the ordinary," Gemma said.

"Fuck." She'd been so sure that had been it. She chewed her thumb. If it wasn't a physical letter, and it wasn't a text—

"Try his emails." She put both hands on the back of Gemma's chair. "Both work and personal."

Gemma didn't argue, but Remi could tell by the set of her shoulders that she didn't believe they would find anything. She typed in silence, glancing up only when Thomas entered the lobby, his brow a thundercloud. "Miss Archer, I can't believe that you—"

"I had a sudden thought about the Graves case; I needed to check it out." She faced him, unable to be apologetic because she prayed she was right.

He shook his head. "You asked to be a part of that consult and then you embarrass me and the company by running out mid-sentence? What do you—"

Gemma's whisper interrupted them. "Oh my God."

Remi spun, immediately turning her attention to Gemma and drowning out Thomas. Gemma had

Desmond's work and home email up, but it was two messages from his work that she'd opened.

One had been sent mid-afternoon on Friday. An image was the first thing Remi saw. It was her and Desmond at lunch, her head thrown back in laughter as he frowned at the mustard on his fingers. The message below was short, but to the point, same in tone as the others:

Drive her away. Or pay the consequence tonight. Last chance.

"The second one?" Remi asked.

Gemma pulled it forward, another image and message. Remi in her white dress, ash-streaked and bloodied. Her eyes were wide as she leaned over Desmond in the parking lot.

You did this.

Thomas swore under his breath, reading over Gemma's shoulder. "Miss Archer—"

"When were they opened the first time?" Remi asked.

Gemma pulled up a line of code, reading something in them that Remi couldn't understand. "It appears he opened both messages early Saturday morning, around three A.M."

He hadn't checked before the party. He'd been in meetings, then getting ready. He hadn't seen them before. Remi stared at the screen but didn't see the messages. Everything he'd said that morning, it had been a ruse, to try to keep her safe. He cared about her enough to try and protect her. He still cared—

"They threatened him." Gemma summarized, halfway out of her seat. "Which means that he…" She stopped, pressing her lips together.

Thomas glanced at her, connecting the dots in the way only he could. "Remi, I didn't know, I'm sorry."

"Don't be," Remi muttered. "You were right. I would've seen this for what it was if I wasn't so…involved."

"But," Gemma said, "this means you can—"

"It means I can't do shit." Remi took a step back and forced herself to focus.

"But if this wasn't his choice—"

"It wasn't. But he's decided to be noble. If I go back and tell him what I know, it's not going to change his mind. It'll make him even more crafty about getting away. He'd walk into the lion's den if it meant protecting someone he cares about."

"He's actually that self-sacrificing?" Thomas asked.

Remi snorted. "He invented the word."

"Then what now?"

She turned on her heel, her phone in her hand, her answer thrown over her shoulder. "I'm gonna keep that stubborn asshole alive so I can kick his ass for being so goddamn noble."

"And then?" Gemma called after her.

Remi didn't answer.

Chapter Twelve

Desmond sat at the piano, tipping the bottle of scotch over his glass. Nothing came out, he sighed, rubbing his eyes. That was the second bottle this week. A long, terrible week, and it was only Thursday.

He hadn't played in a couple of days. But he sat at it every night, watching the darkness inch across his living room. Sometimes he made it to the spare room. Sometimes he didn't.

His phone rang and he glared at it, ignoring the drop in his stomach that came every time he looked at the device. The gnawing chasm of guilt had been there since Saturday. Half came because he hadn't checked his phone before the party. If he had, maybe he could have avoided everything that came after. The other half came from Remi's expression the next morning. He knew he caused that, all by himself.

But it had been the only way. If he'd told her the truth, things would have escalated. He wasn't a complete moron—they were looking to ruin him, not kill him. Which means he wouldn't have been the target of more deadly attacks. They would have gone after Remi. She would have insisted on staying. She would have put herself in harm's way to protect him, and he couldn't...

He refused to be responsible for more of her scars.

That didn't help now, though, as he recalled the

way he'd spoken to her. How he'd brushed her off, how he'd pushed her away, how he'd pretended he didn't care, when in reality…

His gaze dragged toward the bedroom door. The phone rang again, and he flinched, grabbing it. "Hello?"

"Desi."

"Ash." He felt a surge of disappointment at her voice. "What's wrong?"

"Nothing, I…I wanted to check in on you. How are you?"

"I'm fine."

"Are you?"

He ignored that. "It's late, Ash. What's up?"

Ice clinked against glass in the receiver. "You ever miss Dad?"

Desmond hesitated. "For your sake, I wish he was here."

"That's not an answer."

Perhaps it was the drink that made him blunt. Or maybe he was so tired of lying to people. "You had a different relationship with him than I did."

She was quiet, but he heard the ice again. "Did you…wow, this is hard. Did you…did you throw Dad's case?"

He didn't answer, squeezing his eyes shut.

"Desi." Her tone made it clear she already knew.

He rubbed his eyes, the constant burning getting worse. "It was…complicated."

"Wow." She laughed, a harsh, angry sound that sounded familiar. It brought back childhood nightmares of thundering footsteps up the stairs. "You did."

"Who told you?"

"I got a tip from a friend."

"'Course you did." Of course, it would be now. He leaned forward against the piano. "Look, there's a lot you didn't know about him—"

"Fuck you, Desmond."

A dial tone echoed in his ear. He stared at the screen before placing it face down on the piano. "Right."

He'd lost his investigator. He'd lost his sister. He'd lost his...Remi. At this rate, what more did he have to lose? He tipped the empty glass back to his mouth.

What more could he stand to lose?

****

Remi sat on her bed, the glass next to her empty of everything but some melted ice. She had her phone in front of her, watching the little blue dot that denoted Desmond's location. This was textbook unhealthy, but she couldn't help it. If she stared at it long enough, maybe she could figure it out. Her mind fell into the same inescapable loop it had stayed hooked on

First, Desmond's threatened into dropping a case. The only case worth anything is Sam Landon's, though it doesn't match the timing. Vanessa Masoft shoots Landon, but she and Desmond still receive letters. No case matches up with the timing of the first letter. No other cases have any connection to Desmond's father or James Delaney or Landon or Masoft. She should disregard all his cases.

But the first threat was about dropping a case.

Remi rubbed her eyes, then looked around her room, trying to find some connection. Anything at all. But she kept coming up blank. She was missing something important.

Closing her eyes, she sat back, the faint beeping of

Desmond's communicator a comforting sound. She wished she could call him. Talk to him. Try to get him to see that she wasn't about to let him put himself in danger, despite his best efforts.

Try to make him realize that she was going to do everything she could to save him.

God, if the two of them survived this insanity, she was going to lock him in that fucking bedroom for two weeks.

Her phone buzzed, showing a text from Camille.

—How are you?—

—Fine. How's Desmond?—

—Subdued. I believe he and Ashley are on the outs.—

—Why?—

—He won't say. Are you busy tomorrow night?—

She'd be doing the same damn thing every night this week. Why would Saturday be different?

—Funny.—

—Graves has an event downtown. Something for the DA. He says he has to go, but it's a public venue with little security.—

Remi rolled her eyes.

—Did you tell him no?—

—I tried. But he ignored me. He will attend with or without my permission, and I'd rather be on the list to get in.—

"For fuck's sake," she muttered, typing back.

—I'll be there. Send me the address.—

Jesus, this prosecutor was bad for her health.

An address came through from Camille, and Remi came to her feet. She walked out her door, already shouting down the hallway. "Gemma?! I need some creds to get me inside that event. STAT."

****

Desmond dressed with little attention, letting his mind wander. Despite tonight being a special event for his boss, he couldn't muster up any excitement. He glanced at his phone, catching sight of the bags under his eyes in the mirror. Ignoring those, he picked it up, dialing Ashley's number. It went straight to voicemail. Again. He'd been on the receiving end of her cold shoulder before, but this was impressive.

He closed his eyes and let out a sigh. "Ash. It's me. I have this party tonight and wanted you to come. I want to explain everything. So please, meet me there. I've texted you the address. Your name is on the list if you decide to come. Please."

He hung up, staring at the phone as if she'd call back and forgive him. Unlikely.

He went back to his text messages, seeing the most recent ones were from Ashley and Camille. Farther down was Rick. And below that—

He tapped on Remi's name, looking at the contact. If he called, he knew she'd listen. Despite how angry she was, she always listened when he needed her to. And he needed her.

A text came through, and his heart leaped into his throat. But it was Camille, telling him she was downstairs.

Cursing his weakness, he slipped his phone into his pocket. Ignoring the silver of the tracking bracelet still on his wrist, he grabbed his keys. He'd done what he had for a reason. If he ran to her the first second he had doubts, he'd hurt her for nothing. That was unacceptable.

Straightening his jacket, he strode out the door.

****

As she eyed the venue, on the lookout for any weaknesses, Remi's black slacks and white shirt helped her blend in with the waitstaff. With a communicator bug in her ear and her phone in her pocket, she wandered the hotel ballroom, carrying a tray loaded with savory pastries.

In truth, though the lobby's security was lax, the security in the hall was decent. Only people who were on the list were allowed admission. Guards had examined her false staff credentials for a long time. It was only thanks to Gemma's skill that she'd gotten in. Remi caught sight of Camille but did her best to keep out of sight of anyone else by ducking around corners or lifting the tray higher to hide her face.

Still, when she caught sight of Desmond as he greeted a coworker, the breath caught in her chest.

It was the first time she'd seen him since she left his apartment a week ago. He was smiling, but she saw the shadows under his eyes and the tightness in his jaw. Asshole looked like he hadn't been eating, going back to skipping his lunches. Part of her wanted to relish in his obvious suffering. She wanted him to learn his lesson about trying to go at it alone and *trust* her—

But the larger part of her wanted him to be okay, no matter what. He may have been an asshole, but she understood his misguided intentions too well to blame him. Hell, she'd done the same thing before. Didn't mean he was right, but it made it a little harder to be mad at him.

Swallowing back her emotions, she continued to rotate around the room. She avoided Desmond's line of sight as she tried to keep him in hers. As the night wore on, she saw him chatting and drinking with others, as if nothing bothered him.

She also saw how he tended to put himself with his back to a wall or Camille. How he made sure he could see who was approaching. How he carried his drink with him at all times, leaving his palm over it to keep anyone from doctoring it. How his eyes checked the exits, either seeing who came in or making sure he knew the quickest way out. He never kept both hands occupied, always making sure he had one hand free and out of his pocket.

He remembered the crap she'd done and said and taken it to heart. He was taking precautions, despite his former stupidity of driving her away. But even his caution couldn't keep the sick feeling in her stomach away. Remi continued to circle, pinpointing a group of young, near-drunk paralegals. They screamed trouble, but Remi wasn't sure if it was intentional or not.

"Watch the group of drunks near the east bar," she murmured into her communicator.

From across the room, she saw Camille's lips move. "On it."

Remi circled again, watching as Camille and Desmond moved away from the drunks. A sharp cry shattered conversation, and Remi grabbed at the knife at her back. She forced herself to remain still when she saw Camille move toward them. Desmond was off to the side and away from danger.

One of the drunks held a bloody nose, while the other shouted something about making partner at his firm. Remi kept moving, hovering between Camille and Desmond, trying to watch both.

"Everything okay?" she asked.

"Fine." Camille grabbed one by the arm and escorted him to security. "Just idiots."

Most people moved away from the spectacle, staying close enough to watch. The crowd shuffled past Desmond, but no one spoke to him. Remi kept her eyes on him.

****

Desmond rolled his eyes at the fools by the bar. Everyone knew the drinks at these parties were too strong to drink more than two. That's why he'd been drinking soda water for the past three glasses. The others tried to wander past him toward the open-air atrium. He'd sworn to stay away from there, so he moved to the side.

Someone bumped into his shoulder; he glanced down, seeing a piece of paper hit the ground. He knelt, grabbing it. Speaking up, he tried to catch whoever dropped it, but they had vanished in the crowd. "Excuse me, you..." He trailed off, seeing his name on the envelope.

Glancing around, he looked for Camille. She was out of sight, dealing with the idiots and half a crowd between them. Desmond slipped his fingers under the tab and pulled out a single photo. He swallowed, flipping it over and reading the four words.

West exit. Two minutes.

Desmond looked around again, but Camille was still out of sight. He had thirty seconds before she returned, if he was lucky. He glanced at his watch, a minute forty-five.

Putting the picture and his hands in his pockets, he moved toward the bathroom.

****

Remi weaved her way through the crowd, keeping out of sight. It had the added complication of leaving Desmond out of view for a second. When she saw him again, he was walking toward the bathrooms.

"Camille." She tried not to let her nerves come through. "He's heading toward the bathrooms. Location?"

"Still tied up with these idiots. Can get there in a minute."

Remi hesitated. "I'll stay on him." She began to work her way through the party, praying her gut was wrong.

****

Desmond walked past the bathrooms, his hands in his pockets. He felt his phone buzz and picked it up, recognizing the number.

"When you get to the door," a voice said, distorted and unfamiliar, "take off the bracelet. Break your phone and throw both in the dumpster."

"That'll set off an alarm." Desmond was amazed at how controlled he sounded. His hand was shaking as he recalled the photo, the lone figure on the chair—

"A car will pull up. Get in the back seat." The voice continued as if he hadn't spoken at all. "You resist, and we'll—"

"I'm not resisting," Desmond cut in. He wouldn't. Not with the image engrained in his mind.

"You have one minute."

****

Remi stood obscured around the corner, waiting for Desmond to come out of the bathroom. She waited, her stomach somehow migrating into her throat. Something was wrong, something was up. Her instincts were screaming, and she didn't know why.

"Camille." She moved towards the door. "Something's wrong. Get here—"

A shrill beeping echoed from Remi's pocket. A noise she hadn't heard in ages, but one that she was familiar with.

"The tracker's off." Remi ignored any sense of subtlety and slammed the door open. The bathroom was empty. "Fuck, he's not here!"

"Where—"

"West exit is the only way out from here." Remi ran out the door, knocking over a well-dressed gentleman. Another voice clicked onto her communicator.

"Miss Archer, Mr. Graves removed his tracking device and—"

"I know. Gemma, west exit, get a visual now!"

****

The night air was sour with the smell of the dumpster. The chill crept even through Desmond's jacket and shirt, but he wasn't certain it was the weather. He dropped his phone on the ground, stomping down. The screen cracked beneath his heel and went dark.

Desmond dropped the tracking device and his phone into the dumpster, along with the picture. He heard a car approaching, the lights off as it rolled in front of him. The locks clicked in the quiet alley. He reached out to grab the handle, then hesitated.

He glanced behind him at the door, wondering if Camille already knew. He wondered what happened when he took off the communicator. Did Camille get the alert? Did Remi? Was she still looking out for him?

Despite everything he'd done to keep her out of this, part of him still hoped she was watching the tracker. He hoped she'd find him, and he hoped she came nowhere near him.

"I'm sorry," he murmured to no one.

Then he opened the door and slid into the car.

****

Remi threw open the door, her heart in her throat. The disgusting smell of the dumpster hit her. With her stomach already turning, she almost heaved, but forced it back, looking for any sign of—

"Desmond?!" Her voice sounded high and thin, echoing into the night. On anyone else, she'd call it worried. For her, this was terror.

"Gemma?" she asked, her words cracking. "I don't see—do you have a location? A visual? Did you see?"

She jogged to the edge of the alley, but it opened up onto a busy street. She couldn't see anything, no one shouting or yelling, and nothing out of the ordinary.

"His tracker turned off six yards behind you. I don't have a visual. This alley opens up to a street, and it's all a dark zone for cameras. I'm still looking—"

Remi tuned Gemma out, looking six yards behind her. The dumpster.

With no care for her outfit, Remi pulled herself up to look inside. A flash of silver revealed the bracelet and the shattered screen of his phone. Beneath that was a folded piece of paper, sitting on top of the trash bags, still clean. She pulled those three items out and looked around. She couldn't give up, she couldn't stop.

If she stopped, it meant that Desmond was gone, and if he was gone—

Camille burst out of the building. "Remi?"

Grateful for a distraction, she turned. "He left his things, Gemma is still looking so we can—"

"I'm sorry, Miss Archer," Gemma said, "but I didn't see anything."

Remi looked down at the tracker and the cracked phone. The piece of paper fluttered in the breeze, and Remi shifted, opening it up.

"Why would he leave?" Guilt and anger laced the question. "If he said something, I could've—"

Remi stared at the picture. A young woman in a dark room, her hands bound behind her. She flipped it over to the back, seeing the clear-cut instructions. She handed it over to Camille, numb. "They got Ashley."

"Jesus." Camille stared at the image. "And now..."

"They have him."

Chapter Thirteen

Desmond woke with the tastes of cotton and copper choking his mouth. He tried to clear his throat, but it was dry, so very dry. He lay on his side, with cold stone beneath him.

Pushing himself onto his hands and knees, he had to squeeze his eyes shut when nausea rolled through him. As it passed, he tried to recall the last clear thing. He'd gotten into the car, and there had been someone in the backseat with him, someone he didn't know. Then a cloth was shoved over his face. He remembered it was soaked with some cloying substance—and that's all he remembered.

He coughed again and rolled up onto his knees. His suit jacket was gone, his watch and wallet, too. Not that they would have helped.

The stone walls and ceiling denoted some type of factory or parking structure, maybe underground. From somewhere out of sight water dripped in a rhythmic echo. Above, the buzz of a dim lightbulb grated against his headache. No windows, and the door was a heavy piece of metal. Nothing else. Not a cot or a chair. Just stone.

He got to his feet and straightened his shirt as best he could, leaning against the wall. They wanted him to be afraid. Off-balance. Begging. He loved to disappoint.

He waited in silence, staring at the door. Footsteps passed by the door without stopping. They seemed to come in individuals, sometimes in groups. There had to be dozens of people in this building. No one seemed to take issue with an unconscious man being dragged through the halls. Which suggested a gang. Not that it surprised him.

When the door swung open, Desmond didn't blink at the sight of three men who were armed with weapons. One said, "You're awake."

Desmond arched a brow, not honoring that with a reply.

Number two ordered, "Let's go. Boss wants to see you."

"Great." Desmond pushed away from the wall. "Lead the way."

One walked in front; the hoodie he wore was marked with the symbol of a spade. Desmond recognized it. Delaney's Blackheart Gang. The other two, with their guns pointed at his back, wore black T-shirts and had knives sheathed in their belts. As they walked through the bunker, Desmond saw dozens of people lounging in rooms off the hallway. Crates lined the walls, and he noted both drugs and firearms in the open ones. Even if this wasn't Delaney's official headquarters, it was enough evidence to put him behind bars for life.

Which meant no one intended for Desmond to get out of here alive.

****

After draining a concentrated cup of caffeine, Remi dragged herself to her feet. It had been two hours since Desmond's abduction. There'd be nothing at the hotel, his office, or his home. As she entered the conference room at Exceptional Security, vibrating from the extra shot of energy, she found everyone assembled and waiting.

She chewed her lip, waiting for Thomas to speak, but when she looked at him, his eyes were on her. "This is your case, Miss Archer. You take the lead."

Thomas giving up command to anyone was a novelty, but Remi couldn't waste time. She started, caffeine and adrenaline powering her in equal amounts. "Alec, we have Desmond's phone and computer. See what you can pull off of them."

She passed the picture of Ashley to Camille and Farid. "See if you can get a location, details of any kind, based on where or when this might be. If you can't do that, get me what you can off the kind of photo it is."

Turning to Gemma, she said, "Keep all channels open. They're moving him somewhere. Someone's going to see him. Emergency responders who are already looking, a traffic cam, passerby, anything. Work with Camille and local law enforcement to make sure we don't miss anything. If Farid and Cam can narrow down a location, share it with the authorities to tighten the search."

Looking at their newest recruit, Remi felt the guilt of personal and professional failure try to drown her; she shoved it down into a dark corner for later. "Rick, you and Thomas consult to see if there's anything we missed. There's a bunch of shit in my room, so start there."

She exhaled. "Everyone talks to each other. Make sure we all know everything. We never know when something might fill in a blank." With her nod, everyone separated, except Remi and Samara.

Samara's hands were already spread. "Remi, I didn't know Ashley was gone until it was too late. Her tracker was active and in her house. She was checking in on the hour, up 'til Desmond's abduction. Somehow, they took it off without setting off the alarm and—"

"I know. They're good. Maybe they threatened her to keep checking in, or they knew the procedure. Was there anything at her place?"

Samara shook her head. "No. Only the bracelet, which I turned over to Alec. No sign of forced entry, so she either knew him or they took her from somewhere else."

"She knows Delaney," Remi responded. "Come on, you and I are gonna rotate between everybody else, looking for anything that can help us find where he is. The second we find anything, I'll take off running."

With a small nod, Samara fell into step beside Remi as they headed toward the computers and Gemma. "We're gonna find them."

"We'd better."

****

Desmond shifted, trying to get some feeling back into his fingers. The zip ties around his wrists and ankles were tight. Not enough to cut off circulation, but it was close. The chair he'd been tied to was old, but not rickety enough to break if he tipped it over. Besides, he'd rather face Delaney sitting up.

Of course, he'd been sitting here for hours and had yet to see anyone at all. Once the thugs had tied him up here, they'd left him in silence. He'd lost track of time. Whatever drugs they'd used had combined with his exhaustion, and he'd ended up dozing several times. It could have been one hour or twenty-four for all he knew.

This room was sparse, much like the first cell had been. There was a table set up, where a jug of water and an empty glass rested, just out of reach. The rest of the table was covered with a sheet. He knew it was a scare tactic, trying to get him to panic over what lay beneath. So he kept his eyes away from it, paying attention instead to the tripod and camera set up in front of him—and the chair facing him.

When the door behind him creaked open, Desmond did his best not to react. Footsteps echoed against the floor, passed by Desmond's side, stopped in front of him.

"Hello, Desi."

He raised his eyes, unsurprised to find James Delaney in front of him. The pressed suit, beady eyes, thin mustache. He forced himself to stay calm. "Where's my sister?"

He ignored Desmond's question and took a seat. He took the jug of water and poured a glass. After sipping from it, he smacked his lips. "You don't seem surprised to see me."

Desmond smirked, ignoring the way his mouth ached from thirst. "You haven't exactly been subtle."

"No, indeed. In fact." Delaney put the glass down. "I've been quite eager to get you back. I've missed our little games."

At that, Desmond couldn't exactly feign apathy. His breath came a little shorter. Childhood nightmares slammed into his chest as Delaney leaned closer. "Do you know why you were my favorite?"

"What did you want, Delaney? Which case was it that tripped your switch?"

Delaney laughed. "Oh, of course. I should explain." He took another sip of water. "It was never about any one case. If you had dropped Landon's, that would have been convenient, but I didn't care."

Desmond glared at him. "So what? All those games and threats, it was so I'd end up here? Thought your thing was kids."

"It is. But for you, I'd always make an exception. And still, no. That wasn't the goal." Delaney sighed, patting Desmond's hand. It took everything not to flinch away. "It was never about the cases or me. It was about you. I wanted to see how much it took to break you. Would it be the loss of your peace of mind that drove you to recklessness? Your career? Your sister?"

"Where's Ashley?"

Delaney continued as if he hadn't spoken at all. "Imagine my disappointment, Desi. It was a glorified thug that made you turn into a martyr." Delaney's eyes grew a little crueler. "I expected better taste from you than Remi Archer."

"You're one to complain about taste. Where's Ashley?"

"We'll get to that, be patient," Delaney said, his hand on Desmond's knee. "I realized that if you had nothing else, you had her. That would be the thought of a love-struck fool. So we had to get her out of the picture."

"I had other protection. Camille Juma was—"

"It wasn't about the protection, Desi. It was about the *connection*." Delaney gestured between the two of them as if one existed. "That's what I needed to break."

205

"Congratulations," Desmond drawled. "Job well done. Now, where is—"

"No." Delaney interrupted, a frustrated laugh escaping. "No, it wasn't. That's the rub. You drove her off, as planned, but that connection is still there. I know, because of how you look when I say her name. And the way you drank yourself to sleep this week." He paused, something like jealousy appearing on his face. "And the way she chased after you last night, trying to stop you from doing exactly what you did."

Remi was there last night? He didn't let anything show on his face, but from how Delaney was speaking, it was clear he was already aware.

"If love is what's keeping you together, then that's what I'll use to break you," Delaney said.

Desmond didn't bother with a response, his heart hammering against his chest. He prayed that Delaney couldn't hear it.

"No quips? No playful banter?" Delaney lifted his brows. "I'm disappointed."

"If you're so sure you've found my weakness," Desmond managed to say, "then let Ashley go."

"Do you know why I pick children? They're all unique in their way," Delaney said, getting to his feet. "Most are tenacious for a time. Some begin beautiful. Some end up sublime creations out of pain. But you, Desi." He pointed at him with a smile. "You were unique. I never met a child who was so resilient, so unbreakable. I could do anything to you, and you kept coming back."

Desmond's control snapped. "I wasn't coming back. You did."

"You had this…unequivocal hope. You hoped for

someone to save you. You hoped that your father or I would change our minds, make the pain stop." Delaney smiled, stepping over to the table and drawing back the fabric.

Silver implements ranged across the wooden top. Wires, ropes, knives, cables…everything Desmond had experienced at a very young age. Everything that haunted his nights. Everything he worked his entire life to overcome.

"It was partly that hope that made me keep going. How much would it take to break that little boy? It's like your father always said, isn't it? When you back someone into a corner and you take away their safety nets, they'll show you who you are. I want to see who you are, Desi Graves. Without hope, without love, without anything, what will you become?"

Desmond could do nothing but glare. He'd survived this as a child; he'd survive it now. He had to, for Ashley's sake. For Remi's.

"Even now." Delaney chuckled, amazed. "Even *now*, I still see some of that hope in you. Though you still don't understand why this is happening."

"Because you're a psychopath?"

"Perhaps." Delaney smiled. "But the twist is this wasn't my idea."

Behind Desmond, the door opened.

****

Remi was working off of six cups of coffee, two energy drinks, and sheer spite. Gemma had nothing to report from any cameras and local authorities hadn't had any success, either. Working on what he salvaged from the phone, Alec unlocked some of the codes. Farid and Camille had more luck. Based on the background seen in the photo of Ashley, they determined it was an old factory building, and likely by a canal or railway. That put the number in the hundreds that needed to be checked. Gemma was working her way down a list, but it was slow going.

Remi and Samara were on their way to her room when Samara's phone went off. She waved Remi on, taking the call. "It's Ashley's new landlord, I called him earlier."

Remi nodded, heading into her room. Rick and Thomas were in there with her board and information. "Anything?"

Both men looked up at her, and she read the answer on their faces before Thomas spoke. "I'm sorry, Miss Archer."

She sighed, sitting on the edge of her bed and staring at the case board she'd created. So many fucking names and dates and places and—

"Nothing from the landlord," Samara said, coming in. "Anything new here?"

Rick scowled. "Not yet, but—"

Remi stilled as a stray thought passed through her over-stimulated brain. "Shut up. Everyone shut up."

...No, they couldn't have missed that...could they?

"Miss Archer, what—"

"Thomas, shut the fuck up." Remi's eyes went to the board, checking the visitor logs again. Who'd visited the prison, who'd been involved in the cases, who'd known Landon, Delaney and Desmond and...

As her stomach took a giant turn, she spun on her heel and raced for the conference room. She had to be wrong, but the more she thought about it, the more it seemed to be the most obvious answer. And if it was—

If it was, they were completely screwed.

"Camille?!"

She poked her head out as Remi ran up, stumbling back. "Yes—oh, yes?"

"Ashley's picture," Remi said, holding out her hand. "I need to—"

Farid handed it over with a frown. "We looked for everything we could, but there's only so much I can—"

"Shut up," Rick said from behind her. "She's got a thought."

Remi stared at the photo, looking not at the background and floor, but the subject of the picture. The angle of her arms, the bulge in her pocket.

"Oh my God," Remi whispered, her hands shaking.

****

Desmond didn't look away from Delaney until the figure stopped to his right. He didn't need to look away because he knew.

He'd known the moment the door opened. He recognized the smell. He was the one who'd bought her that perfume, after all.

His sister stopped beside his chair.

"Hey, Desi," she said, no tinge of apology in her voice. "Surprised?"

"Honestly?" He was pleased his voice remained calm. She didn't sound like Ashley. It sounded like... "Yes. I thought you were better than Delaney. You were going to school—"

"I dropped out."

"To become what? Delaney's lackey?" It clicked the moment he said it. "You're his new hitwoman. The one who helped Landon."

"Shaping up to be quite the killer." Delaney

preened. "That car bomb was perfectly planted. The letters delivered with surgical skill. And the drive-by? Well, that was…"

Desmond laughed, a hard sound. "I guess I shouldn't be surprised, betrayal is a family trait."

"You're one to talk about betrayal." Ashley's voice rose, shaking. "Mom died, and you turned your back on this family. You sided with the pigs and the lawyers. You put Dad in jail."

He tugged at the restraints, anger driving away the fear. "I was protecting you. I was trying to give you a chance."

"No. You were getting rid of anything that reminded you of our family. Every bit of Dad, you rejected. You locked away anything that made you like him. And you shut out anyone who reminded you of him, including me!" She took another step nearer. "You threw yourself into work and internships and school, and when I needed my brother, you weren't there."

"Everything I did was to help you—"

"Bullshit." Ashley stepped closer. "Everything you did was to make yourself anything other than a Graves. You put away Dad, and his friends, and Delaney's men—"

"I put away monsters."

"What about your girlfriend?" Ashley countered. "You know she's killed, too."

Desmond glared at her and rattled the ties on his chair. "So that justifies this?"

As she leaned toward him, it disconcerted him to see the tears in her eyes. "I want my brother back, Desi. And if this is what it takes…" She sniffed, wiping her nose. "We'll be a family again. You and me, and Rick, and James—"

"If that's what you want, you may as well kill me now."

She drew back, startled. "What?"

"You want to know why I put Everett in jail? Because he let Delaney do that—" He jerked his head at the things on the table. "—when I was a kid. And he would've done it to you, too, if I'd fought back."

"I know."

Desmond drew back, something breaking in him. She knew. She knew, and she still did this to him. She still locked him in here with Delaney. He stared at her, seeing now that tilt of her head, the twist of her lips, that flat stare.

God, she looked just like their father.

Ashley turned to Delaney. "How much time do you need?"

Delaney smiled.

"I'll be back in an hour." She walked past Desmond and headed to the door.

"Ashley." He'd told himself he wouldn't beg, but—

She stopped, and put a hand on his shoulder. "This is for you. You'll see. When there's nothing left, things will be the way they're supposed to be."

"Ashley," Desmond called to her. His eyes were on Delaney, who was staring right back at Desmond, the smile on his face familiar and haunting.

She shut the door, and Delaney's smile widened.

****

"Remi."

A hand shook her shoulder and she jumped, looking over. Samara gave a worn smile, passing her a mug of coffee.

"Anything?" she asked immediately, clearing her throat. She must have fallen asleep at the table. Her eyes still burned, so it hadn't been a long nap.

Samara shook her head. "No. We searched Ashley's old and new apartments. There were photos, cameras, and guns, but nothing that tells us where they are. Alec pulled texts off Desmond's phone, but the tracking on Ashley's is off, and we can't get her records. She must have had them deleted. The emails bounce between so many servers that he can't pinpoint where they came from. Not that they're there now. We don't have Delaney's number, or we'd try that. Gemma is still going down the list, but—"

"But they could be dead ends," she finished. "Keep me updated."

Squeezing her shoulder, Samara left the conference room. Remi sat up amid strewn papers, empty to-go containers, and Alec snoring in the corner. The rest of the team was working and she...she couldn't stop staring at the clock.

Six hours.

It had been six hours, and Remi hadn't found him. She hadn't stopped working, but she couldn't find him. She said she'd always find him.

Farid and Camille filed in, poring over a map of the canals and railways. Remi joined them, looking for leads they hadn't exhausted when Gemma called through the intercom system. "Everyone, report to the conference room immediately."

Remi looked up, Alec rousing at the loud voice. "What's goin' on?"

"I don't know."

The rest of the team filed in, Gemma bringing up the back of the pack. She glanced at Remi, paler than usual. She went to the computer and turned on the projector. "Miss Archer, you've received an email. A video."

The team looked at her, none of them saying a word.

She knew it wasn't something she was going to want to see. She set her jaw. "Play it."

Gemma hesitated, then pressed a button.

Ashley Graves appeared onscreen, staring into the camera. "Hello, Remi. I hope you've figured out my part in this by now. If not…surprise, I guess. I want you to know that I wanted this to turn out differently. I wanted him to choose me over his job. I wanted him to be my brother again."

Remi stared at Ashley, her hands clenching, unclenching. Clenching, unclenching.

"You made that impossible." Ashley glared at her through the camera. "This is on you."

She stepped to the side, and the team reacted. Rick swore, Camille gasped, Alec said, "Oh my God," and looked away, and—

Remi's throat closed up, but she didn't move. She didn't look away. She didn't blink. She had to watch every terrible second because she needed to find something that she could use. She had to, for Desmond's sake.

Tied to a chair, Desmond sagged forward, his head hanging. A faint movement proved he was breathing, but only just. The white shirt he'd worn to the party, stained with old and new blood, hung in shreds and revealed cuts. Long and thin, jagged and deep. Bruises and swelling marked his hands. Marks traversed his arms, vanishing beneath his shirt. They layered over the scars she'd felt on his skin when they'd…

Behind him, James Delaney stood with his hands on Desmond's shoulders.

Rick took a step nearer. "Bastard—"

"I warned you." Ashley turned away from Desmond without any sign of discomfort. "I told you not to let your emotions get in the way, but you didn't listen. So now, this last act is up to you. We'll send you our location tomorrow."

She nodded at Delaney. He grabbed a glass and threw water over Desmond's face.

Desmond coughed and sputtered, his head rolling back. In one eye, the vessels had burst, leaving it red. He glanced at Delaney and Ashley, then saw the camera. Remi watched as it clicked in his head. His jaw tightened, even as he continued to blink, his eyes unfocused. Remi was shaking with the effort of not moving, not responding.

"To clarify, my dear." Delaney smiled at the camera, one hand back on Desmond's shoulder. "The deal is, come and try to rescue him, where we'll kill you and see what exactly breaks loose in Mr. Graves. What kind of man he is when he has nothing? Or, don't come and he dies, and all your hard work goes to waste." He turned to Desmond, who didn't bother to look at Delaney. "Ask your girlfriend to come and rescue you."

Desmond spat at his feet, spattering blood across his pant leg. Delaney sighed, then backhanded Desmond so hard his head snapped back.

Remi didn't even realize she was moving until

Samara grabbed her and held her still. "I'll kill him—"
Remi strained toward the screen as if she could reach
out and grab Delaney and rip him through—

"Go on," Delaney said. "Beg. Plead for her to
come and save you."

Desmond shook his head, dazed, then looked back
at the camera.

"Beg." Delaney's voice grew sharper.

"Say it, you stubborn jackass," Rick hissed under
his breath. "Say it…"

Desmond cracked his neck, a smirk appearing
across his bloodied lips. A familiar, courtroom smirk.

"No, Des…don't." As if he could hear her.

"Archer." Desmond's voice was hoarse and almost
worse than the silence. Remi took a step nearer.

"Remi," Desmond said, his voice growing stronger.
He stared into the screen as if he hadn't endured
everything he had over the past two days. As if he could
see her, he smiled.

"Guns blazing."

Chapter Fourteen

Remi was in her room poring over everything she had. She had to find something they could use to get there faster. She couldn't sit and wait. It was still four hours until midnight, and she couldn't...she couldn't stop.

Because every time she closed her eyes, she saw Desmond staring into the camera. She heard him say her name and—and she wasn't there to help him.

So she threw herself into finding any information that might help narrow down the search. She'd originally told Gemma to repeat the video for details she'd missed, but Thomas and Samara stepped in front of her.

"Miss Archer, you don't—"

"No way," Samara interrupted. "We'll do that. We'll find something. You go...get some rest. We'll call you as soon as something comes up."

She didn't argue, though she'd do nothing of the sort. So she shut the door and tried to find something. She pulled up the files with the photos and threats, desperation sinking in. She grabbed a glass and the bottle of scotch, but only held the liquor for a moment before putting it down. She took the glass to the bathroom to get water, still staring at the files. She put both down to the side, rinsing her face to wake herself up a little bit.

Bent over the sink, she looked up, seeing the bags under her eyes and the deep lines of panic. She shook her head, trying to get ahold of herself. Wiping her face, she went to pick up her things and saw through the glass a distorted version of Ashley's photo. It was the one delivered to Desmond the day of the funeral. It must have been staged since Ashley delivered it.

Numbers swelled and magnified in the glass as she moved, straightening. Remi frowned, placing the glass over the picture of Ashley's phone.

A cell phone number became visible through the magnification.

…they weren't that lucky, were they?

She left the bathroom, photo in hand, and called down the hallway. "Alec?!"

****

Desmond tried to roll away from the hand that pushed his head back. His hands, slick with sweat and blood, slid beneath the ties, but he couldn't move out of reach.

"Relax, Desi. It's me."

He forced his eyes open, seeing Ashley crouching next to him. She held a glass of water to his mouth and though his principles wanted him to refuse, his body wouldn't comply. He guzzled the water until the glass was empty, seeing her a bit more clearly as she set the glass off to the side.

"So." His throat burned. "This is the kind of family time you want, is it?"

"I don't want this. You left me no choice. You always picked the job over me. Even when I was threatened, you—"

"Gave myself up."

"The first threat."

"The fake threat that you delivered." He corrected her, every word causing his throat to ache, but unable to let her get away with more lies.

"You didn't know that. And you still chose to prosecute Landon." She stood, taking the glass back to the table. She set it off to the side, the clean glass very different from the red-tinged implements beside it.

"And Masoft?"

Ashley tilted her head. "An alibi. Delaney and I set her up to think Landon was cheating on her. If you'd dropped the case, he wouldn't have died. Neither would Vanessa."

"I had no proof they wouldn't keep threatening you if I gave in." Desmond tried to make her understand. "If I took Delaney's hitman off the street, it would have weakened him, and lessened his ability to get to you."

Ashley didn't seem to care. "Justify it any way you want. The fact was you killed Dad by sending him to prison—"

"He murdered an innocent man."

Ashley looked over her shoulder at him. "He was our father. I was lost without him. You were always too busy—"

"You never came to me." Desmond interrupted again, tugging at the restraints.

Ashley didn't seem to hear him. "Before Dad died, he got me in touch with James. He helped me. He was there for me. He trained me and taught me, he got me a position in his crew. I was able to get a new apartment. I had everything I wanted, except Dad. So he and I came up with this plan after Dad told me you threw his case. Delaney confirmed it. It took me a week or two to gather the courage, but then I sent that first letter."

"Fine," Desmond said. "You're right. I was a poor excuse for a brother. Kill me, but leave Remi out of it."

Ashley shook her head. "I'm sorry, Desi. I became who I am because you killed someone I loved. You have to go through it, too."

"Kill me. Kill Remi," Desmond said, ignoring the drop in his chest. "It won't change the fact that I'm not Everett. I'll never be."

Ashley dropped her eyes. "It'll be close."

"No, it won't."

Ashley turned away. "There's only two options here, Desi. Remi dies or you do."

The first day Remi had walked him to work, they'd talked about his stalker. What he was like. What lengths he'd go to. Remi had looked away from him, the breeze pushing her hair aside as she said, *"It's gonna be you or him."*

Desmond looked at the woman who was once his sister. "It won't bring Everett back."

She glanced at him, and he was almost grateful to see hurt in her eyes. At least she still felt something. "You've had a long day." She sniffed, changing the subject. "You should get some rest."

She left him alone again, the door creaking shut behind her.

****

They had been that lucky. The number Ashley had dialed was either Delaney's or someone close to him. They'd been able to get a location off of it, an unlisted building amid the canals they'd been searching before.

Remi had committed it to memory, then left the conference room without a word. Now, she stood in the armory, black tactical pants tucked into her boots, three knives apiece in each boot top, extra mags on her belt, alongside her holsters. Her black tank top was untucked to allow freedom of movement and access to the knives on her back. A dual underarm holster over the top of it. She'd pulled her hair back, the half-finger gloves giving her knuckles some protection.

When the door behind her opened, she didn't flinch. "Going to tell me off again?" She loaded her gun without turning. "Try to talk me out of it?"

"Not exactly."

Remi turned, seeing not only Thomas, but Camille, Rick, Samara, Farid, Alec, and Gemma. All in tactical gear, armed up, and ready.

"We said we'd be right behind you," Camille reminded her.

Remi stared at them for a moment, unable to verbalize her gratitude. She settled for a tiny nod. "Thank you."

"We've got your back," Alec said.

Rick cleared his throat. "I'm just going for Graves."

"Are you ready?" Gemma was almost unrecognizable in the tactical gear but looked more comfortable than Remi would have expected.

"Yeah, one thing left," Remi said. "I'll meet you downstairs."

The group trailed down into the lobby hours before Ashley said she'd send the address. At least they'd have the drop on Ashley and Delaney. Remi went to her room, closing the door behind her.

It was quiet, and she paused by the window to glance at the pictures there. Reminders of who she was and who mattered to her, no matter what she did. She committed them to memory, making sure she wouldn't lose herself in what she was about to do.

Remi went into her closet, grabbing a bag from the back and opening it. Her father had sent it to her a while ago, the last bit of her sister's things that he thought she'd like. Inside was a leather jacket. A white leather jacket.

"You look good in white."

Remi pulled it on, stepping out into the hallway. Samara was waiting and arched her brow. "They're gonna see you coming a mile away in that."

Remi gave her a grim smile.

Samara's grin turned wicked. "You want them to see what's coming for them. I like it."

"Let's go."

****

When the door opened next, it was neither Ashley nor Delaney. Desmond lifted his head, looking at the three men. One of them grabbed the back of his chair, turning it toward the door.

"How much longer?" one asked. He was off to the side, and Desmond didn't have the energy to turn.

The one behind Desmond shifted. "Not for another day. Then she's gotta get here. If she comes at all. We're only the first shift."

The third one chuckled. "Oh, she's coming. Didn't you hear? These two are in love." He kicked Desmond's leg; a new burst of pain spiked among the aches. Desmond didn't look at him, keeping his eyes on the door.

"I don't think she's gonna want him now. He's all fucked up." Plastic crackled and Desmond heard the spark of a lighter. "And from what I hear, she's hot."

"Maybe Delaney'll let the gang have some fun."

Desmond blinked, cutting his eyes to the man who'd said that.

He grinned, the thick beard not quite disguising the scar that ran along his cheek and over his eye. "What's the matter? Don't like the thought of someone else taking your stuff?"

Forcing a cold smile, Desmond said, "Trust me, you couldn't handle her."

The other two laughed, while the bearded one flushed in anger. "You piece of shit." He stalked forward and jammed the muzzle of his gun beneath Desmond's chin. Desmond lifted his head, unable to swallow. "We'll see if you're still such a smartass when you're bleeding out and—"

"Stop posturing, Jack," the one next to Desmond said, moving forward. "Delaney told you to leave him alone, so shut up."

"Fuck you," Jack said, lowering the gun from Desmond's throat and stepping up to Derek. "If I wanted to, I'd—"

A distant explosion rattled the building, dust pouring down. Derek and Jack froze, the third man behind them exhaled, smoke swam in a cloud just beneath the ceiling.

Desmond flinched as gunfire began. It was far enough away to sound like faint pops, but it was definitely in or around the building. His guards began to panic.

"Who's that?"

"She's early, how the hell—"

"What's going on out there?"

"—said it wouldn't be for another day."

A voice shouted from the walkie-talkie on one's belt. *"Taking heavy fire, fall back—"* It drowned out in static, but Desmond heard a scream.

"What the hell," Jack whispered. He glanced at the smoker. "Keep him quiet," he said, jerking his head at Desmond.

Desmond felt a knife press below his jaw. The other two aimed their guns at the door, waiting. Gunfire continued over the next several minutes, getting closer and closer.

When it echoed in the hallway outside, Derek cocked his gun, with Jack following suit. They aimed at the door, the faint crackle from the smoker's cigarette the only sound in the room.

A strangled scream cut off outside, followed by a painful thud against the door. Jack jumped, but none of them said a word. The knife pressed a little closer against Desmond's throat. He leaned back, still feeling the pain as the blade cut skin.

Thirty seconds passed, and no one opened the door. The knife at his throat relaxed, a warm, sticky trickle of blood rolling down his neck.

Jack lowered his gun. "Jesus, I thought for sure—"

The door slammed open, and Jack flinched, aiming again. The smoker dropped the knife and scrambled for his gun.

The men around him weren't expecting the figure in the door. A short, young woman, clothed in white and black, with a gun and a bloody blade in her hands. Dangerous and beautiful, protecting and taking vengeance.

His Valkyrie.

He hadn't understood how anyone could have been afraid of Remi. The woman with a weakness for spicy foods and a hatred of formal wear. Who laughed with childlike glee as she teased him. He couldn't reconcile the woman he knew with the one that made Delaney blanch.

He saw it now. Her eyes were flat, her face blank. The black tactical gear was incongruous with the white jacket on her petite frame. She seemed to float on the ground, like a dancer, the weapons in her hands extensions of her arms. He saw the danger now.

So did the men in the room, but the oddity of her confused them. They hesitated. She didn't.

With two quick shots and a flash of silver, all three men dropped. Desmond heard someone choking behind him but couldn't tear his eyes away to look.

Remi shut the door behind her, locking it. She strode in, her eyes assessing the situation. She knelt behind Desmond's chair; he heard a brief struggle. He started to turn, but Remi shook her head. "Don't look."

He did as she said, and the struggle stopped with a wet, cracking sound. She turned, the knife back in her hands. She cut the ties that kept him to the chair at his wrists and ankles. When she finished, she re-sheathed the blade and looked up at him.

That careful blankness was gone, and her eyes glittered with unshed tears. She swallowed, her gaze fixed on him. "Hi."

"Hi." He heard the rasp in his voice.

Her fingers trembled as they started to run over his wounds. She traced the marks on his wrists that'd kept him tied to the chair and the cuts that ran up his arms. Following the scars, she touched his tender shoulder.

Dislocated by Delaney or in his pain-fueled spasms, he didn't remember. She paused at the bruising around his throat.

She drew in a shuddering breath, and that sound broke him more than anything Delaney could have done. He leaned forward, taking her face in his hands. She pressed into his hand, turning her lips into his bloody palm.

"I'm so sorry." Her breath was hot against his cold skin. "I should've been there—"

"No, this was my fault. I can't believe you're here after what I said."

"Of course I'm here." Remi met his eyes. "I told you from the beginning, if you need me, I'm there. Even if you were stupid in trying to do this alone. And even though I was stupid to buy that crap you said." She tried to smile as tears spilled over.

The guilt somehow still hurt more than the physical pain. "I'm sorry."

"Shut up." She helped him to sit straighter, watching his face. "I love you, you pain in the ass. And I'm not going to let you scare me off again."

Desmond grinned, despite the pain bursting across his face. In the desperate hopes he'd allowed over the past week, it was always ages before she'd forgiven him. To hear that she loved him...

Ignoring the bodies around them and his terrible state, he knew he had to tell her. He'd wasted too much time as it was. "I love you."

"I know, why the hell do you think I'm here?" she said, starting to smile as well. She guided him to his feet, the pins and needles from immobility forcing him to take a moment. Once he was up, she ducked under his arm, keeping him steady until he could stand.

"Now what?" he asked.

"Well, I've killed most of the people here. So we're leaving." Pulling a gun out from the holster on her waist, she passed it over to him. "Safety's off. Point and squeeze. Aim—"

"Aim for center mass. I remember." It felt heavier than the first time. Remi stared up at him for a moment, and he frowned. "What?"

"You look hot with a gun."

His grin split his lip again. "Just lead the way, Archer."

With a crooked smile on her face, she pulled away from him, taking a step toward the door. With that brief separation, he couldn't help himself. He grabbed her wrist and tugged her back against him.

The kiss was brief, and it hurt, but it was the kind of pain that came with a healing bruise or ache. It promised better things to come. Remi squeezed his arm, her lips gentle despite the violence he'd seen from her. He knew it was only to save him that she'd gone to these lengths.

Though he couldn't help but feel terrible it had come to this, it was comforting to know that she'd do this to rescue him. It was the first bit of comfort he'd had since he'd convinced her to leave. Desmond held onto that moment, that feeling. He needed it if he was going to make it through the rest of this.

He pulled away, far earlier than he wanted to, and rested his forehead against hers. They both ignored how he trembled. "Did I mention I like the white jacket?"

Remi let out a wet laugh. "I've missed you, hotshot. You ready?"

Desmond swallowed, then nodded. "Ready."

She got to the door, and Desmond watched that change come over her again. How her shoulders drew back; her face smoothed over. She checked her gun with cool efficiency. "I cleared the hallways on my way here, but there could be more. You see movement, you shoot. If they're with us, they'll tell me where they are." She tapped a black piece in her ear. "The rest of the team is out there, securing an exit and working their way in, cleaning up the entirety with local law enforcement. I came straight through."

She unlocked the door and looked at him. "Stay close, stay low. I'll get you out. Understand?"

Though he could still see the mask of the Valkyrie, he saw Remi beneath it all. "Got it."

She grinned and cocked her gun. "Let's go fuck some shit up."

****

Remi kept her head cocked, doing her best to pick up every brief sound that echoed throughout the bunker. She moved silently, her head on a swivel. Behind her, she heard Desmond's lurching footsteps and ragged breaths. Instead of irritating her, as loud companions tended to do, it was soothing. It reminded her that he was still there. Battered to shit and back, but still alive.

When she'd walked into that room and seen him hurt and bloodied, she wanted to tear the building apart. She wanted to kill everyone who'd had a hand in hurting him. She'd also wanted to get him out of there and never have him see any of them again. Regardless of how many escaped in the process, as long as he was safe. Such conflicting emotions, and she wanted both.

Bodies cluttered the floor every few feet, and she

wondered what Desmond thought about it. Her. He didn't say anything, but he couldn't have missed them. Although she worried about what he thought, she had no regrets. They'd gotten between her and Desmond. They'd deserved it.

Desmond's arm brushed the edge of her jacket as if he were afraid she would vanish. How many times had he thought he wasn't going to make it out of here alive? How many times had he thought that she wasn't coming for him?

She shoved those thoughts aside until they were somewhere safer. She focused on the hallway in front of her and the man behind her.

"Samara?" she whispered into the comm. "Status?"

Faint gunfire clicked through as Samara answered. *"Still some holdouts over here, north exit's still blocked. By the time you get here, it'll be clear."*

"On our way."

"You got him?" Rick asked.

"I've got him."

Nothing more was needed. She and Desmond worked their way to the north exit, finding nothing but the ones Remi had already taken care of. It was quiet, but she didn't relax. Not until they were safe.

An exhale of air behind her had her turning, but a gun fired before she saw what caused it. She watched Delaney slide down the wall, red blooming on his stomach. His gun was out of reach, and he started to gag. Desmond stared at him, his gun still aimed. His breath came a little faster, and he wasn't blinking, his eyes stayed on the gang leader. Delaney tried to speak but only gasped.

Remi stepped a little nearer, her gun trained on

Delaney, but with her free hand, she touched Desmond's arm. "Hey."

He flinched, cutting his eyes at her.

She kept her voice quiet and as soft as she could. "You want to end this, you're well within your rights. You can pull the trigger and blow him away."

Desmond looked back at Delaney, but his breathing never slowed. Remi kept her eyes on Desmond, her voice low. "But, once you do it, there's no coming back. You'll always have that with you. Is he worth that?"

He continued to stare at Delaney, who stared right back at him. The look in Delaney's eyes was something almost like...admiration.

Desmond's shoulders softened, and he lowered the gun. "Death is too kind. I'd rather see him rot in a cell for the rest of his life."

God, he was an amazing man. Remi smiled, then picked up the gun that had spun away from Delaney's hand when he fell. Holstering it, she continued forward. She did take a moment to relish in the labored, painful breathing of Delaney behind them.

It took quite a bit of her self-control not to finish Delaney herself. It would be no loss of sleep for her to kill him. She took comfort in the fact that with that gut wound, she wasn't certain Delaney would live to see a court date.

They made their way back through the path Remi had carved. There were fewer and fewer guards this way now. They'd either become engaged with the Exceptional Security or had run when they saw Remi coming. A rumble up ahead made her pause, but they continued forward when silence followed. She tapped the comm. "Samara? We're almost out. Status?"

"Ugh." Samara sounded frustrated. *"Assholes set off a small explosive. Don't have a visual of the exit. Give us a couple of minutes to sort it out."*

Remi turned to relay that to Desmond, but the lights flickered as another explosive went off. Rocks and grit clattered down the small staircase that led up to the exit.

She flinched, guiding Desmond away. "Shit. Come on, we can—"

The echo of footsteps cut her off and she stepped between Desmond and the sound, her gun raised.

"Stay behind me," she ordered. She put her back to the collapsed exit, knowing people wouldn't be coming through that way.

Desmond didn't argue, but she also heard him step out from behind her. Just like that first day. It had to come to this, she'd called it. Him or his stalker.

"Des." Remi didn't care that she was begging. She cocked the gun but knew it was useless. She couldn't fire without hurting Desmond. She couldn't save Desmond without firing. She couldn't do anything but stand between them. She stood between Desmond and Ashley Graves as she appeared from the shadows.

****

This had to be the way it ended.

Desmond stepped to the side, ignoring Remi's annoyed huff of air as she moved to stay between them. He saw Ashley. She had a gun in one hand, a button in the other and seemed unfazed by the sounds of gunfire and the bodies around them.

"You're smarter than I thought," she said, nodding at Remi.

"And you're more batshit than I thought," Remi retorted.

Ashley frowned. "You don't understand—"

"I understand perfectly." Remi took a step closer. Ashley tensed, aiming her gun at Remi. Desmond moved, but Remi held out her free hand, stopping him. "You miss your dad, so you're trying to force Desmond to become him. Here's the thing, though." Remi moved closer. "Your dad was a shithead who beat his kids, killed innocent people, and didn't give a damn about anyone but himself."

"That's not true!" Ashley's gun shook as she aimed it at Remi. Desmond slunk a little closer, not knowing how he could help, but knowing he had to try.

"Of course it's true." Remi's voice was firm, but not cruel. "Otherwise, he never would've sent you to a psychopath like Delaney. He was a cruel, selfish monster, and the only human thing he did was somehow have two decent kids." Remi's gun lowered, and her voice softened. "You don't want your dad. Not really. You want your brother."

"That's what I've been trying to tell him." Ashley looked at Desmond, her eyes wet. He caught her gaze, listening to Remi keep talking, trying anything to get him out alive because that's what she did. She'd do whatever it took. She'd talk down a psychotic family member, walk into a cadre of armed men, put herself between him and a bullet—

"You can't force him to be someone he's not," Remi said. "If you do, then it's not going to be your brother, and you're not going to be happy."

Ashley glanced between them. Desmond held her gaze, hoping that Remi had gotten through. That there was something of his little sister left in this woman. Ashley stared back at him, and he felt his heart sink a little as her glare hardened. "It's not someone he's not. It's his potential." She took a step to the side, facing Desmond full on. "This is the way it has to be."

Remi was rigid between him and Ashley, her arms tense, her gun aimed at Ashley, but he knew it was an empty gesture.

Desmond's gun felt like lead in his hands, cold and wrong. Ashley's eyes narrowed and she took a step forward, lifting the button in her hand. "I've rigged this whole place to blow. You either kill her, or all three of us die, right here." She lifted the button a little higher. "Time to choose, Desi."

He took a step forward, his gun aimed at the ground. "Everything I did was to try and help you. Help us." He moved until he was next to Remi.

"You were trying to get rid of anything that reminded you of our family!"

He stared at her for a long moment. "You're right. I tried to distance myself from what happened. And you were part of that. I'm sorry."

"Sorrys mean nothing, Desi."

Remi snapped. "Oh, grow up!"

"Excuse me?"

Desmond turned to glance at her, reprimanding her under his breath. "Remi."

She ignored him, getting in front of him again—he now saw how that could be annoying.

"You both had shit lives and tried to deal with it on your own. Killing your brother isn't going to fix anything. And killing yourself sure as shit won't do anything either."

"You don't know anything about us!" Ashley shouted, the gun raising toward Remi again. Desmond stepped in the way, but Remi shoved him back, forcing him to stay behind her now. Ashley's hand was shaking.

"No, but I know a lot about killing. And it won't solve your problem."

"You don't know that!" Ashley shouted, tears starting to spill out of her eyes. "Desi, do it!"

"No," Desmond said. "No matter what you do, I'm not Everett. I'm not going to be the kind of man who hurts you." He dropped the gun Remi had given him, drawing Ashley's gaze. "And I'm not the kind of man who lets you hurt her."

"Desi—" She pleaded with tears on her face.

"You either kill me or you don't, Ashley," Desmond said, tired. "But I'm not going to decide for you."

He heard Remi's breath beside him, steady and calm, though he could be condemning them both to death right now. Her hand brushed his shoulder, and she stood next to him.

Ashley's tears continued to fall, and the gun wavered between the two of them. Remi's hand was tight on his shoulder. This could be their last moment, and Desmond couldn't think of a single thing to say that could make this better. He didn't know what to do. So he settled for glancing at her. "I'm sorry."

Remi shot him a small smile. "I'm not."

God, he loved her.

Ashley lowered the gun, cradling the button in her hands. "You'll have thirty seconds to get out after I press this."

"Ash," Desmond said, taking a step forward.

"I'm sorry."

"Ashley!" Desmond took a step nearer, but Remi grabbed his arm.

His sister pressed the button. "Go!" Ashley lifted the gun and waved it toward them. "Go."

"I'm not leaving you."

"Then you're going to die." She looked at the button. "Twenty-five seconds."

"Ashley—"

"Fuck!" Remi shouted, raising her gun and firing off a quick shot. Desmond's heart stuttered, but he saw the graze in Ashley's shoulder. It forced her to drop the gun, and Remi appeared in front of her. Remi swung her fist, and Ashley crumpled. Catching her, Remi slung her over her shoulders and lifted her. She jerked her head down the hall. "Run."

He hesitated, and Remi snapped at him. "You fucking run, Desmond Graves, or I'll shoot you myself! Fifteen seconds." She tapped her ear, somehow holding onto an unconscious Ashley and her gun all the while. "Bombs going off in ten seconds, cover fire northwest exit now!"

Desmond kept time in his head, his feet pounding down the hallway. Pain exploded in his arms, his sides, his chest, his shoulders. He felt like he should be dead, but he kept running—

Ten

He could see the stairwell up ahead, hear gunfire above, and he prayed it was his friends. Because no matter who it was, that's where they were going.

Nine

Remi had caught up and was keeping pace with

him. She could run faster, but she wasn't going to leave him. He saved his breath, knowing he couldn't say anything to convince Remi to go without him. Had he been in her place, he'd do the same thing.

Eight

She was risking her life to save Ashley because she knew how much it would hurt him to leave her behind. The woman who pretended not to give a damn about personal connections was willing to give it all up. He needed to make it through this because he owed Remi everything.

Seven

The stairs were in front of them, and he was hard-pressed not to curse. The first flight hurt, the next one burned, and the following one was excruciating. Remi grabbed his arm, hauling him up the stairs as best she could with her burdens.

Six

The gunfire was getting louder as they approached the top of the stairs. His breath came in short gasps, and the edges of his vision faded.

Five

"When we get out," Remi said, sounding winded herself, "run. Don't stop. Don't look back. Keep running. I'm right behind you."

Four

He could see the door, gunfire so loud he could feel it along his spine. "Remi—"

"I know."

Three

They made it to the door, gunfire lit up the street, coming from both sides. A spray hit the door, and he ducked, hearing Remi curse beneath her breath. He wanted to stop, but Remi shoved him on. "Run!"

Two

He ran as fast as he could, pain lancing through every inch of him. Bullets ricocheted off the ground, and he wasn't certain if they were aiming at them or firing wildly. He kept running, his head hunched down as he focused on getting one foot in front of him, again and again. The pounding of his footsteps was the only sound he could hear amid the gunfire.

Wait, the only sound—

One

He stopped and looked back.

Remi wasn't right behind him.

He saw her, fifteen yards away, still moving, still carrying Ashley, but stumbling. He saw the black pants and shirt, the white jacket—

The burst of red.

She met his eyes, her lips twisted in a smile.

Zero

Chapter Fifteen

The funeral home was almost empty. Candle smoke permeated the air, the employee's hushed whispers the only noise other than faint music. A lone man stood at the casket, staring down at the figure within. Desmond Graves sported a suit, gray instead of black, and no sign of grief upon his face. No sign of any emotion. He tilted his head, taking in the scene.

James Delaney's face looked pale and still. The faint powder of makeup tried to make him presentable. The casket was only half open, an effort to hide the damage from the explosion. Emergency services at the scene couldn't confirm if it had been that or the gunshot that had killed him. Desmond hadn't followed up with them for a concrete answer.

Delaney was dead. That was enough.

Shoving a hand into his pocket, he took one final look. The sight of Delaney's unmoving body confirmed the truth in a way the reports he'd heard hadn't. He'd needed to see it for himself.

It seemed impossible that he was finally, actually dead. One of the figures of his nightmares, about to go in the ground for good. A part of him regretted that he'd never been able to make Delaney squirm in the courtroom. But this was probably better in the long run. No more threats, or hiding, or wondering if Delaney would come after him or anyone he cared about ever again. Letting out a quiet breath, he let go of some of the fear he'd been carrying with him his entire life.

"Good riddance," he murmured.

As Desmond turned away, Rick separated himself from the wall and joined him as they walked out in silence. The bright sunlight made both of them blink, though it wasn't even eleven. Desmond took his time on the steps, his leg still sore, and his left arm of little use. Though he was free of the sling, the doctors warned against exerting it too much. That had proven to be more challenging than he thought, even with an extended vacation from work.

Rick got into the driver's seat as Desmond eased into the passenger side. The dislocated shoulder and stress fractures were the worst of it now. The side effects from the concussion had mostly faded, and most of the smaller cuts had healed. He was recovering well, though he still had a way to go. But he'd walked away from it, which was more than some people.

They got onto the highway, the hum of the wheels the only sound for a while. Then Rick glanced over at him. "How's Ashley?"

"Settling in." Desmond turned to look out the window. "She called yesterday. She sounded tired but okay."

His sister had been released from the hospital a few days before Desmond was discharged. Her wounds weren't as bad—the graze in her arm from Remi's bullet and some smoke inhalation. Upon her release, Thomas had used his connections to have her sent out of town for psychiatric help. They'd agreed that getting her out of the place where she had so many demons might be a better choice. She'd called him every few days once she was there, usually just a short chat to check in with him, but he was grateful. There had been a moment when he'd thought his sister was gone. There seemed to be a chance that they might recover something of a family.

"Let me know when you go out to see her," Rick said.

Desmond nodded, wondering if Rick harbored some of the same guilt he did. He knew he wasn't responsible for Ashley's choices. That didn't make much of a difference in the guilt.

"You coming on Friday?"

Desmond thought it over, considering. Alec had organized another party to celebrate the end of the case, though it was rumored to be somewhat quieter than usual. "I think so."

"Good."

The rest of the ride was quiet. They pulled up outside of Demond's building a few minutes later. He got out, leaning on the door as he said goodbye. "Thanks for the ride."

Rick smiled behind his sunglasses. "Sure, Graves. See you around."

"See you," Desmond answered, closing the door.

With a brief nod at Peter, Desmond took the elevator, the flights of stairs a little much now. He rubbed his eyes when the doors closed, feeling more tired than the short day merited. Recovery was a pain.

The door dinged open, and he stepped out. His eyes still half-closed, he opened his door by muscle memory. Closing it behind him, he locked it, hanging his coat on the hook by the door and not bothering to turn on a light.

The apartment was still and quiet, the mid-morning sun illuminating the living room. Desmond walked past it to his bedroom, shedding the jacket along the way. Hanging it in his closet, he divested himself of the rest of the suit. Exchanging them for a pair of loose sweats, he slid into bed, deciding that sleep would be the best medicine.

A warm body shifted, pressing against his side. Without opening his eyes, Desmond moved his good arm. Remi leaned into his embrace, her head resting on his shoulder. He made sure to keep his arm light on her back, despite her assurances that the burns didn't hurt any longer. Her bare legs tangled with his, the bruises almost gone.

"Is he still dead?" Her words were mumbled, still half-asleep as she wrapped her arm around his chest.

"Still dead."

"Feel better?"

He hesitated, feeling her fingers caress his skin. He felt relieved that Delaney was dead, but that didn't undo everything that happened. His death couldn't erase the memories. But Desmond covered her hand with his, pressing his lips into her hair. He reminded himself that they'd both made it out, alive and together. Turns out the answer was easy.

"Yes."

****

Remi woke up disoriented, her internal clock completely turned around with the recovery. She stretched, the aches and pains helping to wake her even more. Desmond was nowhere in sight, but she didn't worry too much about it. She could smell coffee from the kitchen. Looking around, she saw one of his shirts on the back of the chair and reached to grab it.

"Hey."

Remi looked at the door, drawing her hand back with a smile. Desmond was in the entryway, bearing two mugs of coffee. The sweatpants didn't hide the healing marks around his neck and wrists or the bandages on his arms and chest. But she kept her eyes away from them, knowing that lingering wouldn't help them heal any faster.

"Hi." She settled back into the bed. Her wounds ached, but they were fading, and soon would be just more scars. Desmond joined her, passing the mug over. She sipped it, the warmth almost as soothing as leaning into Desmond's chest. Both of them reclined against the headboard.

His fingers wrapped around a strand of her hair. "Rick asked if we were going to the party on Friday."

Remi scoffed. "I said two weeks, and you can't even make it one."

"Two weeks without leaving the apartment was an insane request."

"Yeah, but it's what I said I would do if I managed to get you through this shit."

"Doesn't make it less insane."

Remi narrowed her eyes, then swung her leg up and over to straddle Desmond's hips without spilling a drop of coffee. "Has it been so bad?"

Desmond's amusement softened, his thumb running over the curve of her cheek. He pulled her closer, pressing a gentle kiss against her lips. When he pulled away, he said, "Yes."

She laughed, rolling off of him and back to her side. She leaned down and grabbed her phone from where it had slid under the bed the night before. As she came back up, she noticed Desmond looking away from her back, his eyes a little tighter. She sighed beneath her breath, hoping it would fade soon.

When Ashley's explosives went off, Remi knew they'd been too close. The lucky shot that had pierced her side had slowed her down enough. Luckily, Desmond hadn't noticed and managed to get far enough away. She'd dropped Ashley, shielding her as best she could and ignoring the wound in her side. The last thing she remembered had been the kiss of flames along her back and shoulders.

The next time she woke, she'd been in the hospital, Desmond in the other bed. They were both hooked up to a slew of machines, gauze covering most of his body and her entire back. Both had healed in leaps and bounds, but the scars remained. Desmond didn't always listen to medical reasoning and was taking too much responsibility for hers.

"I have an invite, and fourteen texts from Alec." She sighed. "And six from Samara saying if we don't go, she's going to make Alec have it here."

"Those monsters," Desmond deadpanned.

She dropped the phone back on the floor, sagging back against the mattress and closing her eyes. "I just want to stay in this bed and rest."

Remi heard the clink of ceramic on wood and looked up to see Desmond looming over her. "Who said you'll get rest here?"

He kissed the juncture of her shoulder and Remi smiled, running her hands through his short hair. Their hospital stay had made any intimacy near impossible, not that either one of them was feeling up to it. When they'd returned to the penthouse, she'd taken three steps in before Desmond had reached for her. He clutched her close as if he were afraid she was going to disappear. It was hurried and desperate, both of them too intent on feeling the other to take much time with it.

The next several days, though, they'd had nothing but time.

Remi had learned that he loved it when she used her nails on his scalp. And that he was ticklish along his ribs, and that he loved holding onto her hips as she—

Well, screw thinking about it.

****

Remi and Desmond arrived fifteen minutes after the party started and parked by the side door. Though neither of them spoke of it, everyone assumed she was moving in with Desmond. Camille had dropped off a few bags of her things the day after the hospital. Though he complained about the mess, he'd smiled when she threw them into the closet. They'd danced around each other for long enough.

The hall was empty, though she still had to swipe her badge to use the elevator. The other guests, much the same as before, would enter through the lobby. They stepped in, the door shutting behind them.

Remi stared ahead, remembering a recent night when this elevator ride had been torturous. The smell of Desmond's cologne, the sound of his breath, and the sight of him in the blue suit had driven her crazy. The one he wore tonight was a dark charcoal gray, and no less appealing. Though it wasn't a white gown this evening, she'd still made an effort. Despite her complaints that she was only going to avoid Alec coming to the apartment. The blue dress was ankle length in the back and a little shorter in the front, flowing and made for dancing. It was sleeveless and low cut while still being appropriate. It had been a gift from Gemma, sent over to her the day after Alec had sent the first invitation. Desmond certainly liked it, though he was unable to show how much since they were running late.

Remi glanced over, seeing Desmond staring. His eyes still darkened for her after almost two weeks of uninterrupted time. She felt the same way. Her stomach tightened as she looked back. The will to resist was more difficult despite, or because of, the fact she now knew how he tasted.

Remi licked her lips, and it seemed to be all the invitation he needed. Desmond leaned down, catching her lips in a heated kiss. She hoped the hitch in her chest never stopped happening when he kissed her. She wanted this feeling forever. His tongue swept against her lips, and she moaned. His suit wrinkled as she pressed against him, grabbing his arms. His hands wrapped around her, heedless of the burns as he pulled her closer. Remi followed him to the side of the elevator, his leg sliding between hers as he bumped against the metal wall.

As one of Desmond's hands started running up along her thigh, she shivered, pulling back to laugh. He grinned, tugging her against him and kissing her again, both of them drunk on one another.

The elevator stopped, and they broke apart. Remi's dress fell back into place, and Desmond straightened his tie. Both were smiling, and as the door opened, Remi fixed the edge of Desmond's collar. She stepped out into the party, Desmond right beside her. She felt his fingers on her wrist and turned her hand to entwine their fingers. Desmond squeezed her hand, and they dove into the fray.

Alec's party, despite being smaller, was still over the top in a different way. He'd taken the rooftop room and converted it once again into more of a lounge. Low couches lined the sides, the music piping through the stereo, but no live band. Food was out and available, and drinks were make-it-yourself. It was still crowded, but there were fewer people than last time, and more of them were familiar to Remi. Liaisons from other security companies were present, wandering around. Remi led the way over to familiar faces in the corner.

"Gotta hand it to you, Alec," she said as they walked over. "You should be a party planner."

"Yeah?" He grinned, pleased. "I do have a knack."

"Forget the whole technological mastermind," Desmond added, "this is your calling."

Alec laughed, then pointed a finger at Desmond. "Tuesday lunch?"

Desmond hesitated, then smiled. "Sure."

"Perfect. I'll meet you outside the Courts building. Food preference?"

"He loves Ethiopian." Remi grinned, ignoring Desmond as he cut his eyes at her, humor dancing within the depths.

"I've got your number," Alec said, "we'll talk."

Desmond nodded, smiling as Camille walked past them to join Rick and Samara at the bar. That left Remi and Desmond with Thomas and Gemma. Farid was busy making a fool of himself on the dance floor with several others.

"You received my email?" Thomas asked Remi.

It had been a summary of events while she was unconscious. The team had performed well, even Alec and Farid. That made this their induction to the Exceptional Security payroll. No one, other than her and Desmond, had suffered any significant injuries. It eased some of Remi's guilt about involving them. "Yeah. You got my report?"

Yes. And you?" Thomas turned to Desmond.

"I received it," Desmond said.

"And?"

Remi looked at him as he stared at Thomas. "I accept."

Thomas gave a rare and genuine smile. "Fantastic. We're lucky to have you on retainer."

Desmond shook the proffered hand and smiled himself. "It should prove interesting, at the very least."

"That's a kind way of phrasing it," Gemma said, resting her hand on Thomas's arm. "I'm going to get a drink."

"I'll join you," Thomas said, nodding at the two of them and then joining the others.

Remi turned to him. "So we're working together, now?"

"On occasion." He tugged her toward the dance floor. Remi smiled, resting one hand over his shoulder and keeping the other entwined with his. He found the small of her back and traced small circles there, holding her close. "Is that okay?"

"Of course. I like working with you." She glanced at the others. "Can't promise these other assholes will be as much fun as me, though."

He laughed, and Remi's smile was a little too soft to be humor. She loved that he was laughing. The first couple of days had been too serious, and too quiet. Laughter was better, and she was determined to get him to laugh every day, even once.

She rested her head against his chest, the same small smile appearing when he pressed his lips into her hair. "I love you," he murmured.

"I love you." She wasn't certain he heard her, but the words vibrated through her chest and into his, so he felt them nonetheless.

The song ended and a throat cleared over the stereos. They parted, seeing Thomas at the front of the room, microphone in hand. "Excuse me, may I have your attention, please?"

The crowd quieted down, and Thomas smiled. "I'm not a fan of speeches, so I'll keep this short. Thank you to all who've come. We're here tonight for several reasons. First, to welcome Mr. Alec Singh and Mr. Farid Nassar to the Exceptions family. They've proven their worth and expertise over the past few weeks, and we're lucky to have them."

Farid and Alec waved in response to the applause, wide grins on both their faces. Remi smothered a sigh that there would be two proverbial puppies in the building.

"I'd also like to welcome Mr. Rick O'Brien. He's worked as a legal investigator for several years but is better suited here. Another worthy addition." Thomas gestured toward the bar, where Rick was still talking with Camille. Both of them ignored Thomas's speech.

Thomas continued, unbothered. "The biggest event has been the closing of our most recent case. Mr. Desmond Graves has agreed to remain on hand. We're grateful to have him as our legal counsel. Especially considering our job requirements and unique… temperaments."

Remi snorted, and Desmond glanced at her with a smile.

"This was a difficult case. We made it through because of our teamwork, dedication, and combination of skills. No one person could have done this, and I am lucky to work with such a talented group." He raised his glass, and Remi smiled up at him, knowing that praise from Thomas was rare indeed.

Thomas took a sip of his drink, then glanced at the man next to Remi. "Did you want to say a few words?"

****

Desmond, girding his metaphorical loins, stepped away from Remi and took the microphone.

"Good evening." He paused, getting his thoughts in order. "I'm certain I'll never be able to repay you for what you did. What you've given me." His eyes surveyed the room, pausing on Rick, who Desmond had seen more in the past month than all last year. On Alec, who had plans to make changes in Desmond's city that he had been working for his whole life. On Farid, who sent dozens of game invites and promised not to relent until he accepted. On Remi, who…

She smiled.

"I'll do my best to return the favor."

He returned the mic to Thomas, who said another quick thank you to everyone. On his way back to Remi's side, Thomas stopped him. "Mr. Graves, a word?"

"Certainly." Desmond stopped, conscious that Remi was closing in on them.

"I know that we are all relieved everything

happened that way it did. For the most part. But we all made mistakes on this case."

Remi had told him how Thomas thought her emotions would complicate things. How he'd doubted her ability to keep a clear head. "Sure."

Remi slid into place beside him, frowning at Thomas.

"I wanted to apologize for that," Thomas said, glancing at Remi, too. "And I wanted to know how you felt about everything."

"What do you mean?"

"I mean, we all did our best. But there's always room for improvement. Do you wish it had ended a different way? That you, or we, had made different choices?"

"A lot of it was out of our control," Desmond said, considering his words. "I regret the pain everyone experienced, but would I have done anything differently?"

Had he made all the right choices?

He shouldn't have lied to Remi to protect her, though he did it with the best of intentions. He shouldn't have tried to drive her away in the beginning. He should have been honest from the get-go. He shouldn't have let himself be distracted by family. He shouldn't have fallen into Delaney's trap. He shouldn't have shot him—but he had.

There were too many regrets there, so he went back to the first question.

Did he wish it had ended differently?

Had this not happened, he would have woken alone today. He would have worked through the day, skipping meals. When he got home, he would have had a glass of scotch, played the piano, and gone to sleep. That's what he'd done every day.

Today, he'd woken to soft, sleep-warm kisses on his face. He'd had a lazy breakfast in sweatpants on the couch, listening to Remi expound on one of her many adventures. He'd worked for a bit, interrupted by a call from Rick. He had to explain to his friend the difference between business casual and black tie. By the time that was over, Remi had ordered lunch and was bringing in cartons of Chinese with a grin. Lunch led to a debate over what qualified as a utensil, which turned into a minor food fight, ending in the bedroom...

Now, he was here. Among friends and with plans for the week. A perfect, challenging, frustrating, amazing woman at his side. There were regrets, of course, but everything he'd done or not done led him to this point.

The answer was simple. "No."

****

It was late that night, or early the next morning. He was wrapped around Remi, his chest against her back and his arms holding her close. One day he might be able to sleep without holding her, but it wasn't going to be soon. He needed that reassurance, that feeling of safety.

"Did you mean what you said?" she murmured, her voice soft in the dark.

Desmond kissed her shoulder, not asking her what she meant. "Yes."

"Even though..." She trailed off, but he felt her fingers run up the bandages on his arm. They were fewer and farther between than they were a week ago, but still present.

"I'm not a fan of words like 'destiny' or 'fate,' " he said, his words muffled by her skin.

Remi rolled over, settling on his arm, her hands against his chest as she met his gaze. Desmond pushed her hair out of her face, studying the lines between her eyes. "I think people are meant for things," he said. "And that our struggles lead us places. Your skills make you uniquely qualified." He smiled, remembering the words she'd chosen that first day on the job. "Your job is what you were meant for, and you thrive there."

He didn't mention the discussions he'd had with Thomas. He wanted Desmond not only for legal counsel, but to help him transfer the company into Remi's name. She would be inheriting Exceptional Security within the next year. She was the heart of the team, reminding them why they did what they did. She led them to where they needed to be, regardless of how difficult the path was. She was an excellent choice.

"My past makes me a...driven lawyer," he added, moving on. "And on their own, they make us incompatible with most people." Desmond drew his hand down her shoulder. His fingers slid along scars and healing bruises to find her palm and entwine their hands. "The journey may have been hell, but it led to this."

"Thought you didn't like destiny." Her eyes were dark as she stared up at him.

"I don't. I am partial to the idea of soulmates."

Remi grinned, that wicked little smile of hers that made his heart leap every time. "Why, Graves, you're a romantic."

"I know what I want, and it's you, Archer. For as long as you'll have me."

Her smile faded, though it wasn't fear on her face. "Was that a proposal?"

He considered it. The ring he'd purchased the day after their release from the hospital was sitting in his nightstand. He wasn't playing around. He wasn't being dramatic. He wanted this life. "Not yet."

Remi's brow lifted as if she were weighing the truth of his words. Finding some answer on his face, Remi kissed him. "I'm not going anywhere, hotshot."

The implied answer out there, Desmond kissed her again. "I wouldn't change a thing, because it led me here."

"Where's here?" she asked, rolling onto her back as he leaned over her.

"To you." He punctuated it with a kiss. "To this." Another kiss. "To us."

"I like the sound of that," she said, already breathless. "Us."

Desmond smiled. "Good. Now, enough talking."

"Fucking *finally.*"

A word about the author...

Michele Leech is a teacher by day and a writer by night. She recently received a degree in library sciences, which just allowed her to find more books to read. When she's not wrangling her daughter or watching movies with her husband, she enjoys reading, playing video games, and daydreaming about her next book.

Thank you for purchasing
this publication of The Wild Rose Press, Inc.

For questions or more information
contact us at
info@thewildrosepress.com.

The Wild Rose Press, Inc.
www.thewildrosepress.com